HER CHRISTMAS WISH

ELLIE ST. CLAIR

Facebook: Ellie St. Clair

Cover by AJF Designs

Do you love historical romance? Receive access to a free ebook, as well as exclusive content such as giveaways, contests, freebies and advance notice of pre-orders through my mailing list!

Sign up here!

Also By Ellie St. Clair

Standalone
Unmasking a Duke
Christmastide with His Countess

Happily Ever After
The Duke She Wished For
Someday Her Duke Will Come
Once Upon a Duke's Dream
He's a Duke, But I Love Him
Loved by the Viscount
Because the Earl Loved Me

Happily Ever After Box Set Books 1-3
Happily Ever After Box Set Books 4-6

Searching Hearts
Duke of Christmas

Quest of Honor
Clue of Affection
Hearts of Trust
Hope of Romance
Promise of Redemption

Searching Hearts Box Set (Books 1-5)

The Unconventional Ladies
Lady of Mystery
Lady of Fortune
Lady of Providence
Lady of Charade

Blooming Brides
A Duke for Daisy
A Marquess for Marigold
An Earl for Iris
A Viscount for Violet

PROLOGUE

Christmas, 1800

"I wish Christmas would last all year long."

"Emily, what a silly thing to say!" her sister Teresa said with an affectionate laugh from her chair across the table.

"I think what Emily means is that the spirit of Christmas would be wonderful to have around us no matter what time of year it is," their mother said gently as Emily passed her the plum pudding with a grateful smile.

"Yes, Teresa, that is exactly it," Emily said with a nod as she dug her spoon into the dessert, searching out one of the little trinkets her mother usually baked into it. "Wouldn't you like plum pudding after dinner every night?"

"I suppose I would," Teresa reluctantly agreed. She was a year younger than Emily, but had recently decided that she was much more mature than her fifteen years.

"And," Teresa said, her eyes gleaming, "then there is much more opportunity to find yourself underneath the mistletoe!"

"I say!" their father, George, declared, his thick eyebrows rising high as he placed his beefy arms on top of the oak table which he had crafted himself. "I hardly think that should be a priority at the moment, young lady."

"Oh, don't worry, Father, Teresa hasn't kissed anyone yet, as much as she'd like to," Emily shared with her family, not caring about the annoyed glare that Teresa sent her way.

"What?" Emily said. "You know we don't keep secrets from one another."

"Perhaps it is time we did," Teresa muttered. "Just because you cannot tell a lie doesn't mean that you should offer the information even if you are not asked."

"Girls," their mother said with the slightest admonishment. "There will be a time for kissing under the mistletoe in a few years. For now, we can enjoy *creating* the mistletoe rather than spending any time underneath it."

"The Nicholls family is coming to call later," Teresa said with a mischievous grin. "Perhaps James and Emily might find their way beneath it."

"James and I are just friends, Teresa, as you well know," Emily said with a roll of her eyes, though she wondered if Teresa could ever be right. Emily and James had made a pact not long ago. If they were not married by their twenty-first birthdays, they would marry one another. Now *that* was one piece of information that Emily wasn't about to offer, and she was sure it would never come to pass. That was a full five years away, and she was sure she would find someone to truly love by then. What she wouldn't do to have a love like that of her parents. She looked between the two of them with a small smile. Even throughout this very dinner tonight, she noted her father staring at her mother now and again as though he had just seen the most beautiful woman in the world for the first

2

time. It was so lovely it nearly brought a tear to Emily's eye.

Not that she would say anything. Teresa would only take it as another opportunity to tease her. Emily longed for romance with a man nearly as much as she yearned for the day she would become a mother.

All of the children present tonight at the church had been angelic — well, except for the Smith boy who had raced from one end of the aisle to the other until the Smiths had to leave. But other than that, the service had been resplendent, with candles lit throughout the small building, and the dozens of people within singing together in harmony.

"Why *is* Christmas so special?" Emily asked now, looking from one of her parents to the other. "Why have we always placed it in such high regard?"

Her father placed his knife and fork down on his plate as he gave her his full attention.

"In our family, Christmas has always been a special time of year," he said. "It was at Christmas that your mother and I met and we have always made sure to carry on the same traditions year after year. Tradition can cause rather warm feelings to arise, as it brings back memories. All of this is in addition to what we truly celebrate, of course — the birth of our Savior."

"The birth of any baby is cause to celebrate," her mother, Mary, added. "But the birth of Baby Jesus makes it that much more special."

Emily nodded. This, they discussed every Christmas, so they would never lose sight of the true meaning of this time of year. She sighed wistfully. James had a baby sister, and Emily doted on her. It was partially why she enjoyed spending time with him — she could see the baby as well.

"I never want this to change," she said, looking around the table at her family as the Yule Log cracked in the fireplace. "I love this time we are able to spend together. This day is so very special, and I cannot imagine it without any of you."

Her mother bestowed a smile upon her.

"Someday everything will be different," Mary said. "The two of you will marry and have families of your own, and then you will begin new traditions."

"But perhaps part of that tradition can be all of us being together." Emily looked around the table. As much as she looked forward to a family of her own, she could hardly imagine leaving this one. "Please, let us make that a promise? That, no matter what, we will be together at Christmastide. Perhaps it might not be on Christmas Day or New Year's Day, but at some point in the season, we must come together and share this moment. Do you promise?"

She looked at each of them intently.

"Of course, if that is what you continue to wish," her mother said with a smile, and her father nodded his agreement. Emily looked over at Teresa.

Despite being adamant that she was far past anything overly sentimental or childish, Teresa nodded.

"Yes, Em, we will be together. I promise."

Emily smiled and tucked back into her plate of food.

As long as they were together, Christmas would forevermore hold this special feeling in her heart. Of that, she was sure.

1

November, 1816

"Now close your eyes, take the spoon, stir clockwise, and — most importantly — make your wish!"

Henrietta beamed up at Emily before she squeezed her eyes tightly shut, grasped the spoon in her little hand, and began to stir. Her lips moved as she whispered, "I wish for a new doll. One with real hair the color of sunshine and eyes painted as blue as the sky."

Emily smiled at the innocent wish of a child before Henrietta reluctantly passed the spoon over to her brother, Michael, who was rolling his eyes.

"It's supposed to be a *secret* wish, Hen," he said as he took the spoon.

He was not quite as enthusiastic about his turn to stir, for he considered himself far above the chore of preparing Christmas pudding, but that didn't stop him from closing his eyes and creasing his forehead in concentration as he made his wish.

"Oh, Mrs. Nicholls, how I love Stir-Up Day," Henrietta said, looking up at Emily with eyes as blue as those of the doll she wished for.

"It is a fun day, isn't it, love?" Emily said with a soft smile as she remembered how equally special she had found Stir-Up Day when she was young.

"*Especially* because it means Christmas is coming soon," Henrietta said excitedly. "Don't you wish we could eat the pudding *today*? It's so hard to wait."

Her tone went from excited to wistful as she sighed heavily and Emily had to hold in her laughter at the dramatics.

"I understand, Henrietta, but then once the day arrives, the pudding is that much more special," she explained, and Henrietta nodded in understanding.

"Will you stay with us this year for Christmas, Mrs. Nicholls? We missed you last year."

"I know, Henrietta, and I would love to be with you as well, but this is when I go home to see my own family. And you are able to spend all of your days with your parents."

Henrietta sighed once more.

"I know. It's just that Mother and Father are so *boring*."

Emily had to bite her lip to maintain her straight face, even as she heard the cook snort from her place at the stove.

"Now, Henrietta, your parents are not at all boring," Emily managed once she ensured she had composed herself. "They simply have many responsibilities to see to, is all. Now, shall we return upstairs? There is some time for us to have a quick play outside before your lessons if you'd like."

That caught Michael's attention, and he hurried out of the kitchen and up the stairs as fast as he could. Emily smiled farewell at the cook before taking Henrietta's hand and following her other charge up the stairs. While she enjoyed bringing the children down to bake from time to time, she certainly didn't envy the servants who spent their lives below stairs. The kitchen was spacious and well-maintained, but no matter the time of year, it was always sweltering and far too dark for her liking.

Emily craved the open air and was always relieved when the Winmere family retired to their country manor. She had been governess to their son and daughter for nearly two years now, and while Lord and Lady Coningsby may be rather boring, as their own daughter described them, Emily certainly had nothing untoward to say about them. They allowed her a great deal of freedom to deal with her charges as she saw fit, and she knew that they deeply loved their children — they just didn't seem to quite understand how to best relate to them.

"Mrs. Nicholls?" Henrietta tugged at her hand. "Can we go see the ballroom? The maids are beginning to prepare it for the party next week, and I cannot wait to see what it looks like!"

"I'm not sure there is much to be seen quite yet," Emily said, as the affair, which was to signify the Winmeres' return to the country, was nearly a week away. "But yes, we can go look. For a minute, is all."

"Wonderful!" Henrietta said as she raced to the door of the ballroom, her eyes wide as she looked around the extravagant hall.

While Emily, of course, had to maintain a much more stoic reserve, she could certainly understand the girl's excitement. The ballroom was stunning on its own, with golden arches and mosaics of angels frolicking in the clouds cascading across the ceiling and down the walls. The floor mirrored the shape of the paintings above it, and intricate Corinthian columns lined the room. Advent was about to begin, and Emily knew there would soon be lush greenery strewn about the room to signify the coming of the Christmas season.

She sighed as she looked around at the maids scurrying throughout the ballroom in preparation, and then managed a quick smile when she caught the eye of the housekeeper, who was overseeing the entire affair. What would it be like, Emily wondered, to be a guest at such an event? She closed her eyes as she remembered her own secret wish when it had been her turn to stir the pudding. The wish had been unbidden, but she had pictured herself dressed in the finest gold ball gown, with a low bosom of lace and a flowing skirt that draped about her ankles. In her vision, she had been without her spectacles, which was rather silly as she wouldn't have been able to see a foot in front of her without them. Her hair was pulled back in a style that Lady Coningsby would be proud to wear, with soft ringlets, as plain a color as it was, gently brushing the side of her face.

Emily shook her head to rid herself of such a thought. She was a governess, and she was lucky to hold such a position. Her younger sister, Teresa, had been searching for such a post, but after she had spent two months avoiding the groping hands of her previous employer, she was now living with their parents until she could find another position, or if she could, a husband.

"Mrs. Nicholls?"

Emily looked down to find that Henrietta was tugging on her hand once more.

"Michael is already outside, heading to the stable. Can we fetch our cloaks now?"

"Of course," Emily said with a smile, telling herself not to be so silly as she followed Henrietta out the door. She was more fortunate than she could imagine, and she'd best remember such a thing. She had a post any governess would envy. She earned enough to help support her parents as best she could. And she had the ability to care for lovely children. Did she wish, deep in her heart, that she had her own to care for? Of course she did. But this was as close as she was ever going to come.

THE RED BRICK facade loomed above Charles Blythe, Earl of Doverton, as he stood in front of it with a walking stick in one hand and a hat in the other. A frozen breeze brushed over him carrying the whispers of winter upon it, causing him to shiver despite his heavy cloak made of some of the finest material to be found in London.

His valet stood behind him, waiting nervously with Charles' valise in hand, rocking back and forth from one foot to the other as though unsure of what exactly to do with it while his employer stood immobile in front of his own estate.

It wasn't the grand estate, with wings stretching east and west amongst the plains surrounding them, that scared Charles. It was what waited inside — or, rather, *who* waited inside.

"Lord Doverton!" the butler finally made the decision for him and opened the front door, shouting his greeting to be heard. "We are pleased to welcome you home. How was London?"

"Just fine," Charles said with a nod as he chose the left

curved staircase and began the climb up the narrow stone steps. "Good to see you, Toller, as always."

It was true. The jovial butler had been with their family some twenty-five years now. He could hardly believe it had been that long. But time had a way of slipping by, he reflected as he passed Toller his hat and cloak and continued on through the entrance and into the grandiose marble hall.

"If you would like to see Lady Margaret, she is in the music room," Toller said, taking his hat and cloak.

"The music room?"

"Yes. She has become quite taken with the pianoforte as of late."

Something else that his own butler knew while Charles had no idea of such a thing. Should he go in there? Or should he have a drink first to fortify himself? Why was he being so ridiculous?

Because she had stolen his heart, that was why. And the last time he had attempted to make known his affections, she had rejected him and all that he could offer her, choosing instead to stay within the hard shell she had built around herself.

"Does she know that I am here?" Charles asked the graying butler, providing him only the briefest of glances so that Toller wouldn't see how affected he was by this reunion.

"She knows that you are arriving this evening, my lord," Toller responded before leaving the room.

Charles squared his shoulders and steeled his resolve as he strode through the opulent marble hall and the domed saloon, down the curved corridor, and finally into the music room in the left wing of the house. He recalled his wife had been musically inclined, though they had not spent nearly enough time together for him to become overly familiar with her accomplishments.

The music reached him long before he neared the room itself. The tinkle of the piano keys floated down through the manor — his *home*, though it hadn't felt like it for many years — and he followed the sound until finally, he found himself standing in front of the rather unfamiliar room. He took a hesitant step across the threshold of the doorway now, knowing she sensed him when her fingers suddenly stilled, her body going rigid as silence filled the air.

There she sat, as still and silent as one of the many marble busts that adorned his home. Without the music, the air became pregnant with the tension that had always existed between the two of them.

Her hair was as dark as he remembered it, glistening in the light of the intricate chandelier above her head. He couldn't say he remembered the light fixture. But then, he hadn't visited this room in the past two years since the death of his wife, and he certainly hadn't frequented it often before then.

Finally, she turned, those aquamarine eyes, identical to the ones that mocked him daily from the mirror, piercing into him. She was even more beautiful than he remembered.

His daughter.

"Margaret? I'm home," he finally said, stating the obvious, his words echoing through the silence of the room. When her only response was a curt nod before she turned back to the instrument, he continued. "Do you have nothing to say to your father after all this time?"

He cringed at the harshness that came across upon the words. The girl would take it personally, and yet it was himself that he was upset with. It had been far too long since he had last seen her. But he was afraid. He, an earl who sat in the House of Lords, who made decisions that affected the lives of not only those who worked for him or who lived off his land, but who lived throughout this country, had no idea what to say to an eight-year-old slip of a girl.

And she knew it.

2

One Week Later

L ord and Lady Coningsby had outdone themselves once again.

Charles stood at the top of the stairs as he looked at the ballroom before him. He was announced — alone — though no one paid much attention. There were glances from some of the eligible young women and their mothers, of course, but most who would be invited tonight had already done their utmost to capture his attention.

While Charles appreciated the effort, he simply wasn't interested. Soon enough, he would find someone suitable. He just hadn't the energy at the moment.

"Doverton!" Lord Coningsby exclaimed as Charles reached the bottom of the stairs. "It's good to see you again, old chap. It has been a minute, has it not?"

Charles smiled at the man who stood next to the stair-well with his wife on his arm. The two of them had found contentment with one another, which Charles looked upon with both pleasure for his friend and his own bit of envy. If only he and Miriam had found the same with one another... but that no longer mattered, so why dwell on the past?

"I have been in London for a few months now and only returned a week ago," Charles said, coming back to the moment and assuming his practiced smile for occasions such as this. "I would have called upon you earlier, but I knew you would be deep in preparations for this evening."

Coningsby laughed heartily. "Alexandra here was, of course, but I would have welcomed the distraction. You would think this would become easier year after year, but alas, it remains as much work as ever. Now, there are plenty here who are looking forward to speaking with you."

"My family?" Charles asked with a raised eyebrow. "I see Anita over there, as well as Katrina."

"Of course," Coningsby said with the slightest of smirks, for he knew Charles' true feelings regarding his cousins, "but I was speaking of a few young ladies. You aren't getting any younger, you know, Doverton, and since Miriam has been gone some time now— ouch!"

Were they speaking of another subject, Charles would have enjoyed Lady Coningsby's unsubtle reproach to her husband's topic of conversation, but he would prefer that none of them continued to speak of this.

"I may not be getting any younger, but it seems the eligible women are," Charles said, filling the silence as he surveyed the room. "Why, many of the women looking my way are young enough to be my daughter."

"*That* is certainly no way to create a romantic sentiment," said Coningsby, chuckling. "But you do have your succession to think of."

Charles sighed.

"That, my friend, is my greatest concern."

Coningsby nodded in understanding before Charles took his leave to find himself a drink, hearing Lady Coningsby chastising her husband as he walked away. Coningsby had never had much ability to determine just when he should speak and of what, but Charles actually enjoyed that about the man. It was far better to know what to expect.

He had just taken his first sip of brandy, welcoming its warm sensation sliding down his throat, when he heard his name being called. Recognizing the voice, he prepared himself so that when he turned, his distaste would not be evident within his expression.

Apparently, he was not as successful as he would have thought.

"Coningsby serving cheap brandy?" his cousin Edward asked as he approached. Charles attempted to sink into the wall behind him, but that only served to back him into the stone, where a tall angel with pink wings awaited.

Despite Edward being the same age as him, the two of them had never gotten on well. Perhaps it was because Edward had coveted everything Charles had ever called his own — including Miriam.

Unfortunately, the title, the estate, and all that it entailed would fall to Edward were anything to ever happen to Charles, for he had no other siblings and Edward was the closest blood relative.

Charles hadn't been disappointed in having a daughter. In fact, he could still remember the euphoria, the love that he had never before felt tugging at his heart the moment he held the tiny baby in his arms.

But that was before. Before the miscarriages. Before Miriam's icy politeness grew into a hostility that barred him from entering her room. Before she had not only kept his own child from him but had turned her against him.

Before Charles had to come to terms with the fact that he would never have a son, and all would, one day, be lost.

There hadn't been anything to be done about it. And then Miriam had died, and Charles couldn't imagine himself going through all of that once more, though of all the responsibilities he held, perhaps seeing to his line was the greatest. He had never been able to let go of his father's teachings — of the importance of ensuring the male line survived.

He would find a wife. A young, fertile wife who would provide him with plenty of sons. He just had to be sure of one thing — after the pain of losing his daughter's affections, he would never fall in love again.

"I NEED MY DOLL, Holly, Mrs. Nicholls," Henrietta said in a quiet voice, her voluminous blue eyes pleading with Emily.

Emily sighed inwardly. She seemed to spend more time searching for Henrietta's well-loved wooden doll than she did looking after the children.

"And where is it, darling?" Emily asked with as much patience as she could muster as she crouched down in front of the girl. Henrietta bit her lip and hung her head so that she didn't have to meet Emily's eyes.

"Henrietta?"

"Just tell her, Hen," Michael offered from across the room, looking up from his book. They were sitting in the nursery, though the room was no longer fitting for young children. Emily had reformatted it into a library of sorts, and a secondary place where they could work on their lessons when the actual library was unavailable.

"I can only find it if you tell me where it is," Emily said after taking a deep breath. "You know how important it is to be honest with one another."

"The ballroom," Henrietta whispered, looking up at Emily with regret in her eyes. "Behind the last row of chairs in the corner beside the angel with the long pink wings."

"The ballroom? Good heavens, Henrietta, what is it doing in there?"

"I wanted to see the ballroom beautifully decorated before the party began, and I must have left my doll in the corner when the housekeeper caught me sneaking through."

"Henrietta, we shall have to get it tomorrow. You know the ballroom is currently filled with all of your parents' friends."

"Oh, please, Mrs. Nicholls, we *must* find it tonight! I cannot sleep without Holly, you know I simply cannot! And what if someone takes her? She could be gone by morning!"

Emily pushed a few stray strands of hair back from her forehead. She certainly had no wish to enter the ballroom, full of the viscount and viscountess' noble friends, but Henrietta had a point. If that doll was lost, there would be tears for many nights to come. Better to suffer through a moment of embarrassment to save both Henrietta and herself some pain later on.

"Very well," she said with a sigh. "Sit down, now. I'll be right back. Then it is straight to bed — no stalling, all right?"

"Oh, thank you, Mrs. Nicholls," Henrietta said, all smiles now. "I do love you, you know."

"And I, you. Now, I'll be right back."

Emily hurried down the long corridor, her hand on the balcony, before reaching the staircase to the ground floor. The symphony of music grew ever louder as she took one stair after another before she finally reached the landing. Here, maids and footmen scurried back and forth, refilling drinks, adding food to the sideboard, and fetching cloaks and hats.

Hopefully, she could find her way through the throng without being noticed. She supposed she looked enough like any other servant who was moving amongst the guests, though she was dressed slightly better than the maids who served food and drink.

She tiptoed to the door of the ballroom, although it was not as though she had to be quiet — somehow it made her feel less likely to be noticed. The pink angel was painted upon the wall in the farthest corner, of course. Emily decided she would keep to the outskirts of the ballroom so as not to be observed, particularly by Lord and Lady Coningsby.

Emily had to admit that she could see what had drawn Henrietta to the room. It was stunning as it was, but even more so with white lilies from the conservatory placed in lavish vases ornamenting the room, along with laurel, holly, ivy, and pine, already draped around the columns in preparation for the coming Christmas season.

If that wasn't enough, the people who filled it nearly overwhelmed her senses. Her ears rang and she was nearly dizzy from the scents and sights. Women were draped in extravagant gowns of every color, jewels dripping from their ears and down their necks. Their hair was curled and twisted into knots more elaborate than anything Emily had ever seen. Her entire family could probably live off the cost of one of those dresses for an entire year, she thought ruefully, but then shook her head.

Enough of that. She was lucky to be here and to work for such people.

Emily pushed her spectacles back up her nose as she returned her focus to finding Emily's doll instead of ogling the guests of her employer's ball.

The wooden doll. She would find it quickly, and then back upstairs she would go — to her rightful place.

"Hello, Edward," Charles greeted his cousin.

Unfortunately, Edward looked much like him, enough that the two of them had been mistaken for brothers many times before.

Fortunately, they were not.

"Charles," Edward said with a wide grin. "I'm happy to see you. Our visits are much too seldom."

Or too frequent.

"What keeps you busy these days, Edward?" Charles asked, bringing his drink to his lips.

"This and that. Keeping my wife happy. Raising my children. Doing what I can to prepare Thaddeus for his inheritance."

"Oh? Did you come into money recently?" Charles asked dryly, to which Edward laughed.

"I mean the title, Charles! You've but a daughter, and it looks to me like there will not be another Lady Doverton judging from the interest — or lack of — you have shown any lady. Just as well. I will look after the title someday, Charles, as will Thaddeus. Ah, don't look so glum about it. We'll take good care of things for you. In fact, Leticia has already begun to plan her renovations to Ravenport — as countess or dowager."

There had already been more than enough renovations to Ravenport for his liking thanks to his wife. He wasn't going to settle for any more — particularly from Leticia. He had seen Edward's home, and he had no desire for his manor to follow suit.

"I did not realize my demise was imminent."

"No, no, Charles, of course not," chuckled Edward. "However, Thaddeus and I have had many discussions about the manor. While you do your best, I'm sure, you are slightly too... generous. Your servants seem as well off as you, and sometimes I question whether your tenants are working for you, or if you are working for your tenants!"

Charles' teeth ground together of their own accord at the thought of his lands and his people in the hands of Edward or Thaddeus. Edward's son was a rake of the worst sort — Charles had heard rumors that the man not only found himself in the beds of quite a number of women, but some were less willing than others. Good Lord, what would happen to his lands in the hands of either of the two of these men? It had taken long enough for Charles to correct many of his own father's mistakes. It pained him to think of all he had done erased once more.

"Thinking of the good times to come, Charles?" Edward drawled out, a gleam in his eye.

Charles straightened and looked Edward right in the eye.

"Actually, as it happens, I am to be married very soon."

He wasn't sure where those words had come from. He most definitely was *not* planning on marrying soon. Or at all. But he had no desire to allow Edward to continue to believe he would be taking his place. It was time to put to an end any mention of these plans.

"You are not getting married," Edward said with a smirk. "I am sure it would be on the tongues of all the London gossips."

"We have kept things rather quiet," Charles said as confidently as he could, creating his story as he spoke. "It is a second marriage for both of us, you see."

"Ah," Edward said with a gleam in his eye, clearly still not believing Charles. "And just who is the lucky lady? I am surprised that she is not here with you."

"But of course she is," Charles said smoothly. "She will return soon, I am sure."

"Oh, come, Charles, you are making this all up," Edward said with a laugh. "You have never been much of a liar. Just tell the truth of it, man, and be done with it. Is it really such a horrible thought that I might inherit your land?"

It really was.

"My soon-to-be-bride is here. Of course she is," Charles said, turning his neck, catching sight of a blond head coming straight toward him. A quick glance told him she didn't seem to be anyone he knew. "Here she is now."

He reached out and took the lady's hand just as she was about to pass by him, hoping that whoever she was, she would go along with his ploy for just a few minutes. Then he would figure something else out later on, but for now, he had to preserve his honor in front of his cousin.

The cousin whose face was currently frozen in shock.

Charles hastily turned around. Once he caught sight of the woman, he couldn't turn away.

The first thing to capture Charles' attention was her dress. It was... serviceable, if he was being generous with his description. A navy, boxy creation, it was difficult to determine her shape beneath it. Next came her hair. A sandy blond, it was pulled tightly back away from her head, and on her nose perched a pair of spectacles. Through them, her wide brown eyes stared at him incredulously, her fingers nervously touching her throat.

Well, like it or not, this was the woman he had chosen to be his wife.

For the next few minutes, at least.

3

———

So much for not being noticed.

"Can I help you, my lord?" she asked the elegantly dressed man who currently held her hand hostage. His expression mirrored her own shock.

His face suddenly broke out into a surprisingly wide yet clearly forced grin, his teeth straight and even. He had a square jaw, a slightly crooked patrician nose, and blue eyes that were, strangely enough, the same color as those of the angel painted on the wall behind him — the one with the pink wings.

"You can always help me, darling," he said, confusing Emily all the more. Was his mind addled? He didn't look it, what with his elegant navy jacket, immaculate cravat, and well-fitting — perhaps *too* well-fitting — breeches. But why else would a man such as he be calling her his darling?

He squeezed her hand tightly for a few seconds, and when she returned her gaze to his face, it almost seemed as though he was looking at her imploringly, very similar to little Henrietta as she had requested her little doll. His eyes flicked over in the direction of the man next to him, and he tilted his head toward him ever so slightly. Did he want the man to believe his words then?

Emily felt warmth — which would mean plenty of color — rushing to her cheeks. If he wanted her to play along with this charade for a few moments, he might be in trouble. She had never been a competent liar. In fact, she never even attempted a fib in front of her family, for they knew instantly when she wasn't telling the truth. Her face would flush a bright red, a rash breaking out on her chest and upper arms. It was much easier to simply always speak the truth. And besides that, this man would have to be a fool were he to believe that she would ever even be speaking to a gentleman such as this one, let alone be anything more to him.

"This is Edward — Mr. Blythe," the man continued, gesturing with his free hand toward his companion, who looked very much like him, though Mr. Blythe's nose had not been broken, as this man's clearly had, and he was slightly smaller in stature. "My cousin. I was just telling him about you."

Mr. Blythe stared at her for a moment, confusion in his eyes that likely mirrored her own. Then he shocked her by beginning to laugh. He chuckled long and loud enough to attract the attention of others nearby, and Emily looked from one side to the other as she tried to determine the best way to slink out of the ballroom as quickly as she had entered before Lord or Lady Coningsby saw her.

"Oh, Charles, you never had much of a sense of humor, but this is a good one!" Mr. Blythe said, slapping his hand upon his thigh. "Why, you nearly had me going there for a moment. That this creature could be your bride. Thank you, miss, for playing along, but you may run along now."

A riot of emotions began to coil through Emily. At first,

she was shocked at the fact that this man — Charles, apparently his name was — would have ever named *her* as his bride. But then anger began to coil deep within her belly at the fact they were clearly having some fun at her expense.

"I can assure you, Mr. Blythe, that I have no desire to be a part of anyone's joke," she said with a carefully controlled tone, directing her words to this Charles as much as to his cousin.

Charles turned a frosty gaze on Mr. Blythe.

"Apologize for insulting my intended, Edward."

"Come, Charles—"

"Apologize."

Edward looked from one of them to the other, as though attempting to determine whether or not Charles was serious. Charles kept his hardened gaze on Edward.

"I, ah, I'm sorry. Miss..." Edward said, though still obviously incredulous.

"Mrs. Nicholls."

"Mrs?" his eyebrows shot up.

"I'm a widow."

"Of course. Mrs. Nicholls, my deepest apologies," he said, though the skeptical look remained on his face as his eyes moved up and down Emily's frame. "I will be seeing you at Christmas, then?"

"Christmas?"

"Of course. Charles hasn't told you about our Christmas tradition? We all gather at the family home — Ravenport Hall — and have a joyous twelve days together."

It was his turn to grin now as he looked at her once more. "It shall be quite a revelation."

"Yes, I'm sure," she said, forcing a smile onto her lips before turning to her apparent husband-to-be.

But first Edward had one more thing to say.

"I suppose I do understand this, after all."

"Excuse me?" she asked, sensing that she likely didn't want to know what he had to say, but unable to ask anyway.

"Why, Charles has been hesitant in taking another wife, as he feels all the eligible women are far too young for him — children, he calls them. Well, that certainly isn't the case with you!"

Emily had enough of this conversation. She wasn't sure whether they were both making a joke of her, but she didn't care who they were or what class they might be. She was not going to stand here and allow herself to be humiliated.

She would love to tell them just exactly what she thought, but that would be going a touch too far. She had enough sense to hold her tongue in order to keep her employment.

Cheeks flaming hot, she looked around her for the treasure she sought. She spied the doll under a chair next to them. She turned from the men without another word, grabbed it, and stalked from the ballroom as fast as she could, leaving the fools behind her.

"IT SEEMS that your betrothed is quite upset with you, Charles," Edward said, eyeing Charles with a smirk. "Now, why ever might that be?"

"I would assume it would be because you insulted her," Charles said, shame overcoming him at putting the woman, whoever she was, in such a position. He had, for once, allowed his cousin to get the better of him and cause a momentary lapse in judgment. If Charles had not stopped her, she would never have had to listen to Edward and all of his harsh words against her. "Now, if you will excuse me, I'd best go speak with her."

He would apologize, explain as best he could, and then allow the woman to be on her way. As for Christmas... well, perhaps he would have to cancel the family gathering this year. For he had no wish to prove Edward right, but nor would he be able to find a fitting wife in four weeks.

"Charles, Charles. Do not tell me you actually thought I would believe that woman is to be your wife?" Edward said mockingly. "For if that is the case, you really have become desperate. Her?"

"Yes," Charles answered grimly, not revealing his lie now. Besides that, whether or not she truly was his betrothed, who was Edward to mock the lady? "Her."

"Well, I look forward to introducing her to the rest of the family this Christmas," Edward said, his grin now stretching ear to ear as he clasped his hands behind his back and preened. "You may want to pay for a gown or two for her though, if she can't afford her own. Poor woman looks like she's been wearing that dress for decades. Of course, if she does not attend, I will delight in sharing this farce with the rest of the family, you know that, do you not? Oh, and Charles? It would be lovely if your daughter would deign to enter the same room as the rest of us this year. It's too bad we must suffer from the loss of her presence just because she hates you so. Very well, then. I'll be seeing you."

And with that, he winked at Charles and then strode off to meet another acquaintance. Charles sighed. This would not do. This would not do at all.

He couldn't think of anything else but to convince the woman to carry on the charade through Christmas. He knew it was foolish. But there was one thing he would hold onto, and that was his pride.

Charles looked around the room, seeking out the woman, but she was nowhere to be found. Where in the devil had she gone to? It shouldn't be hard to find her drab navy dress amongst the swirling colors the rest of the women wore. It was as though she had vanished into nothingness. He swore, about to find his host to ask if he knew who she was, but just then he caught a glimpse of navy retreating from the far side of the ballroom. He strode across the floor as fast as he could without breaking into a run, pushing past guests he normally would have stopped to speak with.

He had just stepped through the doors when he heard a tread on the stairs above him, and he looked up to see her stepping off the landing onto the first floor of the estate. Where was she going? Charles was going to call out to her, but then thought better of it and began to ascend the stairs after her, curious to see just what she was doing in the house of his friend.

This could explain her attire. Perhaps she wasn't a guest, but here to steal from Lord Coningsby. Oh, Edward would certainly enjoy that one, if it turned out to be the truth.

She walked confidently down the corridor as though she knew exactly where she was going, and let herself into a room on the far end, shutting the door behind her. When Charles reached it, he pressed his ear against it and heard voices inside, though he had no idea who she would be talking to. Did she have an assignation with a gentleman? That would be the utmost embarrassment, to walk in on the two of them, particularly after he had just announced her as his fiancée.

He turned the doorknob ever so slowly so as not to make a sound, then gently pushed the door open a crack so that he could hear better and possibly see what — or who — was within.

"Mrs. Nicholls, you found it!"

Charles' jaw dropped open.

"Of course I did. From now on, we keep the doll within this room or in your arms, all right?"

"Yes, Mrs. Nicholls. Thank you for finding her."

"Into bed with you now, love," Mrs. Nicholls said, taking the girl's hand and leading her toward a connecting door. "And you, too, Michael."

"I have but one more chapter left, Mrs. Nicholls," the boy responded from his window seat.

"Take it to bed, then, along with one of the candles and finish it there. It's growing late."

The boy nodded, pushing himself up off the cushions before walking through the door on the other side that led to a second room.

Charles pushed the door open a crack wider so that he could see through the nursery and into the room beyond where Mrs. Nicholls — who must be the governess, he realized with a shock — was sitting on the edge of a bed.

She leaned down and kissed the little girl on the forehead before tucking the blankets in around her and the doll that, Charles surmised, was the cause of the woman's appearance in the ballroom.

"Now, close your eyes and dream good dreams tonight, love."

"I will. Goodnight Mrs. Nicholls."

"Goodnight, Henrietta."

Charles retreated back a step into the corridor as Mrs. Nicholls rose and returned to the nursery.

"Goodnight, Michael!" he heard her call out, and

Charles stepped back so that he was leaning against the wall opposite the door.

She was in the hallway and had already closed the door behind her when she saw him.

"Oh!" she exclaimed, one of her hands coming to her chest. "My goodness, I didn't see you there." After she regained her composure, her eyes narrowed as she studied him. "And just what *are* you doing up here, my lord? Would you like to further mock me?"

"I wished to speak to you," he explained simply. "And so I followed you."

"I doubt there is anything more that you and I have to say to one another," she said dubiously though not maliciously, and he took that as a hopeful sign.

"Actually, there is," he said, following her when she began to walk down the hall. "I have to apologize."

"Do you now?"

"I apologize for putting you in an awkward position," he began, one hand behind his back while the other gestured toward her. "I needed to appear betrothed for but a moment, and I selected the first woman I laid eyes on who I wasn't acquainted with."

She smiled grimly.

"How unfortunate for you that you chose the governess."

"How was I to know that the governess would be in the ballroom?"

She finally stopped and turned to him, her hands on her hips.

"You are correct. I never should have been there. I was retrieving a lost wooden doll and came upon you at the wrong time, it seems. But there I was, caught by you and your — cousin, was it? Now, tell me, my lord," she continued, "who are you and what is it you want from me?"

They were fair questions. One was easily answered.

"I am Charles Blythe. The Earl of Doverton."

"Oh," she said, her pink lips rounding with the syllable. "I see."

"I thank you for not disputing my ruse. Edward can be rather... facetious, and I simply wanted to prove him wrong about something. I am sorry that he insulted you. I can assure you, that was never my intent."

"I am not *that* old," she muttered.

"There is no shame in aging," he said, but at her dark look, he hurriedly continued, "not that you appear to be."

She studied him for a moment longer before surprising him with a rueful chuckle.

"One cannot help the effects of the passage of time, I'm afraid. However, your cousin is right in that I am no young maiden. In fact, I will be three-and-thirty this year. You have now apologized, my lord, which is *very* noble of you, and all is forgiven. I am quite tired so I will be going to my own bed now. Enjoy your party."

She placed her hand on the doorknob behind her, and he realized they now must be in front of her own room.

"Actually, there is one more thing," he said, holding up a finger. "I must ask you for a favor. And not a small one at that."

"What is it?" she asked with raised eyebrows.

"Would you celebrate Christmas with me?"

4

"You cannot be serious."

Emily knew she shouldn't speak such a way to an earl, but once again, she worried that he might be slightly addled.

"You now know I am a governess," she continued, "and you would ask me to come to Christmas with you?"

"Yes," he nodded. "You know now what my cousin is expecting of us. I would feel a fool to invite my family and not have you there, now that I have claimed you as my wife-to-be. I will make some excuse following Christmas and will find another to wed."

"You do know that choosing a bride is not like buying a house or a new jacket," she said dryly. "One does have to agree."

"Of course," he said, his face turning red. "Though when one is an earl..."

"People typically agree regardless?" she asked, just one eyebrow rising now. "This all seems rather extreme."

He lifted a shoulder. "Perhaps."

"Well, I am sorry, my lord, but I already have plans this Christmas."

"I can speak with Coningsby if necessary, although I would prefer to keep this between us."

"I am actually taking time away at Christmas," she said, her heart already warming at the thought. "It is the only time of the year that I am away from the children, and thankfully, Lord and Lady Coningsby accommodate me most wonderfully. I return home to see my own family, and nothing is more important to me than being with them through Christmastide."

"Do you have children of your own?"

"No," she said, her heart aching anew at the thought. "No children. My husband, James, passed a few years ago. I am, however, quite close with my parents and my sister."

He rubbed his knuckles over his chin. "Is there nothing I can do to convince you?"

"No, my lord."

"What is your price?"

"Excuse me?"

"How much money would it take to convince you to join me?"

Heat rose in Emily's cheeks at the suggestion.

"You think you can just pay for whatever it is you need, with no regard for others or what might have meaning to them? I can assure you, my lord, that you cannot buy time with my family."

"What about buy time *for* your family?" he asked, his rather piercing blue eyes boring into her.

"Whatever do you mean?"

"You may not want the money, Mrs. Nicholls, but I would pay you handsomely. Enough that you could support your family, allowing them to live with additional means.

What would you say to that? Would one hundred pounds suit?"

It's was now Emily's jaw that dropped open.

"You cannot be serious. That is more than I would make over two years."

"I am very serious. Come to Ravenport Hall two days prior to Christmas Eve, Mrs. Nicholls. It will provide us time to come to know one another better before my family arrives. I will be waiting for you, and will pay you upon your departure."

Emily opened her mouth to deny him once more, but no sound came out. For as much as her heart longed to say no, to tell him that she was going to see her family this Christmas and nothing would deter her, her mind told her that would be foolish. Her father was sick, her sister currently out of work after she left her own governess post when the master of the house became more interested in how she could service him rather than look after his children. With this money, Emily would no longer have to worry about her family, and would not have to work so hard to look after them all.

It was a sacrifice she just might have to make.

"I'll think about it," she said softly, and then turned, opened the door to her room, and closed it on the earl.

THREE WEEKS later

EMILY SWALLOWED HARD as she stood in front of the imposing estate, staring upward at the six-columned Corinthian portico. The rusticated stone invited her to reach out and touch each unique piece, unlike the smooth-dressed stone that extended above on what she assumed were the upper corridors. The middle section of the house would have been enough to intimidate any visitor, but to the east and to the west stretched imposing wings that mirrored one another in design.

She took a deep breath as the cold wind hit her face, her cloak billowing out behind her. She had walked a long three miles after disembarking from the stagecoach that took her as far as Duxford. She knew she could have written ahead and arranged for someone from the house to have greeted her and conveyed her here, but she had no idea until the very last moment as to whether she was going to go through with this; nor did she know what exactly to say in her letter.

Even now, she shuddered to think of what was to come over the next week or however long she would be expected to remain — that part had yet to be determined, but she did hope she would be able to spend a few days with her family before she was to return to her employment.

She had briefly stopped in their village on the way here, had hugged and cried with her parents and sister over their separation and far-too-brief reunion before she continued on. They were understanding, though she didn't tell them the entire story. Only that she had commitments this year and wouldn't be able to spend the entire Christmastide with them — all true. She had to wipe away tears for most of the short journey here, while many on the stagecoach watched her with strange expressions, though two kind women had offered her sympathetic smiles and a hand-kerchief.

Well, she'd best climb this staircase before she had second thoughts. If it wouldn't have been another three-mile walk the other way, she very likely would turn around, saying goodbye to the small fortune that awaited her. But as it was, she was simply too cold.

Come, Emily, you are made of sterner stuff than this, she told herself as she climbed one side of the curved staircase before lifting the great U-shaped knocker and letting it fall on the door.

Her knock was soon answered by a short man, with stiff, curly gray hair standing out at odd angles from his very round head.

"Hello, there," he said with a smile, as though a governess with spectacles and attire from seasons long-ago called upon the front door of the estate every day.

"Have you been expecting me?" she couldn't help but ask, and he wore a look of bemusement, as though he didn't want to insult her.

"We are expecting many guests over the next couple of weeks, of course," he said, standing up on his toes so that he could better see over her shoulder beyond her. "For whom do you work? We just weren't expecting anyone to arrive so *soon*, is all."

A flood of heated embarrassment rushed through Emily.

"I ah, that is, I am not one of the servants."

"Oh no?" The man bit his lip, looking quite perturbed. "Who are you here to see?"

"Lord Doverton," she said, cringing at the butler's surprise. "Perhaps I have made a mistake. Clearly, his invitation was a fleeting one. I shall just leave. Thank you, sir."

She turned to go, when suddenly his rather loud "'oooh," caught her attention and she returned her focus to the house.

"You are Mrs. *Nicholls*."

"I am."

"Ah, Lord Doverton did tell us that you were coming. He simply did not explain..."

That she did not look like a lady, perhaps? Emily said nothing, allowing the butler to come to his own conclusions.

"Forgetful me! Yes, of course, I will take you to Lord Doverton. Come, come."

Emily was wearing her best dress and yet even the butler took her to be a servant. Lovely.

The moment he turned, Emily was able to see the entirety of the room in front of her. It took her breath away. Alabaster columns held up the high-coved cornices above them, niches in the wall displaying the finest of statues, with gray paintings above them. Their lack of color was more than atoned for by the intricately patterned marble floors, which were highlighted by sun streaming through the skylights overhead.

Emily found it difficult to keep up with the man's short yet quick strides as he led her through the room that didn't seem to serve any purpose besides greeting the estate's visitors. She was able to take a breath when they finally turned into what she assumed was a drawing room, and it was equally as beautiful.

She was surrounded by a sea of blue-and-white papered walls, with an ornate chandelier descending from the middle of the room, around which were blue-and-gold settees. In the middle, pink upholstered chairs surrounded a table, all which seemed so delicate that she was hesitant to sit down upon any of them.

"Would you like anything to drink?"

Emily jumped but was pleased she didn't emit a sound at the voice that came from beside the white-marbled fireplace. She finally located its owner.

"Lord Doverton," she said, a hand upon her breast. "You have startled me once more."

"It seems I have a knack for doing so," he drawled, pushing himself away from the wall and walking toward her. "So, would you?"

"Would I what?" she asked, feeling like a fool over the fact she could hardly form a coherent sentence in front of the man. She was many things, but one thing she was not, was stupid.

"Would you care for a drink?" he asked again, his crystal blue eyes, the color of the walls of this drawing room, holding her captive.

"Ah, yes, I would," she said. If there was ever a time a drink was called for, now was it. "Brandy, please."

He raised his thick eyebrows at that, but he inclined his head. "Brandy it is, then."

It was then that Emily noticed the butler remained by the entrance, and he quickly poured her drink before he disappeared through the drawing-room doors, pulling them closed behind him.

"Sit, please," Lord Doverton said, waving a hand around the room. "Wherever you would like."

"Perhaps by the fire," she said, and he nodded, pulling two of the chairs closer to the flames, probably the only warmth in the room, which included the man himself in Emily's estimation. He was certainly the proper English lord, but she wished he would show just an inkling of emotion as it would make her feel somewhat more comfortable. He reminded her of this drawing room, which was beautiful, but not a room she could imagine living in.

"You have quite the entrance hall," she remarked, and he emitted a quick laugh, though one without much humor in it. She wondered if he ever truly laughed. He was certainly a proud man, to the extremes he was going in order to see through this entire charade.

"I do. My ancestors were rather ostentatious. It's beautiful, to be sure, but utterly useless," he said, surprising her. "However, nothing can be done about it now but to enjoy it. I far prefer the family rooms, which are in the east wing. I will show you to them later."

A tremor of nervousness fluttered in her stomach at the mention of the family wing — where apparently she would be staying.

"Your butler thought I was a maid," she finally blurted out, and the earl shrugged a shoulder nonchalantly.

"Of course he did. Look what you are wearing."

"It's my favorite dress!" she said, standing and holding her arms out to the side as though to show off the garment. Then she looked down at the high-necked gray dress she had made herself, and she quickly lowered her arms once more. Perhaps he had a point.

"Clearly," he muttered, and she narrowed her eyes at him. "Not to worry, it will be rectified," he continued without any further explanation. "Now, as to what to say to the family."

"This, I am curious to hear," she said.

"My family likely wouldn't believe that I am to wed a governess," he began, and she stiffened. "I apologize if that offends you, but it is the truth. However, you cannot be of noble blood, for then my cousins would likely be looking up your family connections in Debrett's."

"My grandfather was a baronet."

"I see."

He tapped his index finger against his chin as he contemplated.

"We shall say that we met at a ball, as you are an

acquaintance of a friend of mine. 'Tis the truth, anyway. Where are you from?"

"Newport."

"Ah, not far from here."

"No. I was able to stop on my way to explain to my parents why I would not be joining them for Christmastide."

"Very well," he said. "That all makes sense to me, so it should be enough for everyone else. Now, come, I will show you to your room myself."

Emily nodded as she stood, nearly choking as she threw back the remainder of her brandy, and then followed the man without emotion from the room.

5

Charles led the woman down the curved corridor that led to the family rooms. When his housekeeper had asked him where to put her, he hadn't been entirely sure what to say, as it was a rather unorthodox situation. Mrs. Nicholls couldn't stay in the rooms of the lady of the manor, of course, and she also wasn't a young lady with a chaperone. He had decided on the guest bedroom nearest the family bedrooms. She would be close to Margaret, which somehow made it seem more proper.

Margaret. By God, he hadn't thought of how he was going to explain Mrs. Nicholls to the girl. He couldn't very well tell her that he was going to be married, and then change his mind a few weeks later. She was perceptive, however, so she would know something was unusual about the situation. A friend, he decided. That would have to be enough.

The lady following him was rather quiet, for the moment at least, which Charles appreciated. She wasn't one of those blathering idiots who talked about nothing for hours on end.

"Here we are," he said when he finally reached the door he had instructed to be made up as her room. "I hope you should find everything acceptable."

He held the door open for her and she stepped inside, the scent of rosemary washing over him as she passed him. He heard an audible gasp, and he frowned, unsure what to make of it.

"Is something amiss?"

"Amiss?" she repeated, turning to him, her brown eyes wide. "This is... well, it is the most spectacular bedroom I have ever seen."

He looked past her into the room, attempting to see it through her eyes. It was fine enough, he supposed, and what he would consider a rather comfortable room. He actually couldn't recall the last time he had stepped foot in one of the guest bedrooms of his estate, as he really had no reason to. This one was covered in yellow paper with red ribbons and leaves all over the walls, the yellow canopy and bedspread finished with crimson piping. There was a small fireplace, currently lit, and a vanity tucked into the corner. Above the hearth hung a painting of one of his ancestors, who was wearing a dress that matched the room and was clearly the inspiration for it. He didn't think this room was Miriam's doing, for she had preferred dull colors, much like Mrs. Nicholls' dress. He hoped she wasn't the same. Not that it mattered, for it wasn't as though she would be here long enough to suggest any redecorating.

"I'm glad you will enjoy it," he said, urgent to leave now for he was unsure what more they could discuss in the entryway to her bedroom. "New dresses are awaiting you in the wardrobe."

"New dresses?"

"Yes, well, I was optimistic that you would actually come to join us. Forgive me once more, but I didn't think you would possess the type of gowns that one might expect a lady to wear as dinner attire."

"Your family gatherings appear to be much different than my own," she said with a wry grin, and he nodded, though secretly he wondered if perhaps hers were more enjoyable than his. It seemed that all his family managed to do was determine who was currently the one the rest of them should be most envious of as they all sought to impress one another with their current acquaintances and invitations. "Tell me, what traditions do you include in your celebrations?"

"We attend Christmas mass, of course, and have dinner together," he said, wondering why she would ask. "The family stays a couple of weeks. We host a rather large celebration on Twelfth Night."

"What about choosing the Yule Log?" she implored. "Or decorating your home with greenery? Or mistletoe?"

"The servants do all of that," he said, as he was becoming increasingly worried about the fact that she was here to pose as his betrothed. He had thought that, as a governess she would, at the very least, be familiar with the ways of noble families, but it seemed she didn't quite understand. "We enjoy it all, of course — with the exception of mistletoe. It is a family gathering, and in my family, kissing wouldn't exactly be welcomed."

"Not even between married couples?"

He shook his head as he thought of his own marriage. "Most decidedly not."

"Oh," she said, sinking into the soft mattress as though the thought of it all had exhausted her. "That is rather sad."

"It is still an enjoyable time of year," he said, regarding the woman who, he was beginning to realize, was quite ill-suited to the task put before her. "Quite festive, and all that."

She nodded, but he could tell she was skeptical.

"You shall see soon enough, I suppose," he said with a nod from where he still stood near the doorway. "Now, betrothed or not, I suppose I really shouldn't be alone in your chamber with you. I do hope you enjoy the dresses."

He looked around the room to see where the butler had placed her belongings. "Where are your bags?"

She waved toward the wardrobe, next to which sat a serviceable though rather worn black carrying case. "I've just the one."

"Good heavens," he said, thankful that he had gone ahead and ordered the dresses. He hadn't been sure what to do. He knew it would have been an egregious expense if she hadn't arrived, but he couldn't take the chance she wouldn't. He had to guess on her size, and the modiste had been quite displeased with him, for he was far too general about the measurements. There had been no time for custom dresses but she was able to make some alterations and send them to him just in time.

"I shall see you in the morning," he said, stepping out with a hand on the doorknob. "The housekeeper has assigned a lady's maid to see to you. She will be in shortly with a tray for you as well, for we have already eaten. Goodnight, Mrs. Nicholls."

"Goodnight, my lord," he heard her respond as he began to shut the door behind him before remembering one more thing.

"Oh, and Mrs. Nicholls?"

"Yes?"

"My lord will never do for a future husband. Charles is fine."

"Very well... Charles," he heard her murmur, and then he started down the hallway, taking a large breath.

This would either be the worst idea he had ever had or the best. He just had no idea which it was yet.

The sun struck Emily full in the face the next morning, and she jumped from her bed, realizing she must have slept quite late. As soon as her feet touched the plush Turkish rug on the floor, however, she suddenly remembered that she was no longer in the small, bare yet clean and serviceable room next door to the nursery.

She was at Ravenport Hall, the estate of the Earl of Doverton, who, for all intents and purposes, was her fiancé for the next fortnight. She shook her head, still in disbelief at all that had transpired.

She had been so tired last night — from both the walk and her nerves — that she had collapsed into bed almost immediately after her maid had left her. Jenny, her name was, and a rather talkative young girl, which Emily didn't mind. The more Jenny spoke, the more Emily learned about the household and the Earl of Doverton.

There was a knock at the door, and the girl entered the room but a few moments later.

"Mrs. Nicholls, good morning," she said pleasantly. "I wasn't sure when you would wake, but I see that I'm right on time."

Emily smiled her welcome as she slipped on the wrapper that she had brought with her.

"If you have other duties to see to, Jenny, I am fine. I honestly don't need someone to help me dress."

"No?" Jenny asked, raising her eyebrows. "Well, how do you suppose you are going to fasten all of those buttons?"

"Buttons?"

"Why, yes. All of your morning dresses have a good deal in the back. It would take you some time to fasten yourself. When I was putting them away before you arrived, I was admiring them. You're a lucky woman, to have a man who would buy such a wardrobe for you."

Emily had been so tired, she hadn't even looked at the dresses to which the earl had referenced. She advanced toward the wardrobe now with some trepidation.

When she opened it, she let out a startled gasp. It seemed that she would forever be surprised throughout this Christmas adventure.

For there within was a selection of dresses that she knew even Lady Coningsby would envy. They all seemed to be created out of the finest of muslins, satins, and silks. She was pleased to see that they were not pastels and bright colors that a young debutante would wear, but rather hues such as deep crimsons and royal blues that would far better suit her.

"These are beautiful," she breathed, and Jenny nodded as she joined her beside the open door.

"They truly are," she said with a smile, "and you will look a *beautiful* sight in them."

"Oh," laughed Emily, "I'm not sure about that."

"Why ever not?" asked Jenny. "You've a fine figure, and what I wouldn't give for hair the color of yours."

"Of mine? It's nothing to speak of really. It cannot quite make up its mind as to what color it is."

"I would say it is the color of wheat stalks," she said, and Emily blushed.

"You are too kind."

"Well, what do you say we try one on?" she asked, and Emily nodded. "I suppose we should," she said, taking a deep breath, as this was all becoming so very real.

And so it was an hour later that she ventured down to the dining room for breakfast. Never in her life had it taken her an hour to get ready, but then never before had she been served warm chocolate in her room while she prepared for the day, and never before had anyone curled ringlets in her hair, nor take minutes to simply do up the back of a gown — and a morning gown at that. She could admit, however, that she had also never felt quite so beautiful. She had chosen a cream dress, the morning dresses being much lighter, and covered it with a shawl in case there was a chill in the air, these estates being rather drafty in her experience.

Following Jenny's directions, she had found the dining room by following the curved corridor once more, passing through what appeared to be a study, and then crossing the great marble hall.

"Here we are," she murmured as she entered, finding a sideboard full of an assortment of breakfast foods, including eggs, toast, sausages, and bread and jam of all sorts. The Earl was not, apparently, awake yet, or perhaps he had already been, for the dining room was empty save two footmen who stood at the side as still as statues.

"Good morning," she said with a smile, and they looked at her in surprise.

"Good morning, my lady," one finally said, and once he spoke she realized he was rather handsome, though young.

"Just Mrs. Nicholls, for I am not a lady," she said as she began to fill her plate. "My, this is lovely."

She typically ate with the children, but there were also more people residing within Lord and Lady Coningsby's estate. Were there other guests already in residence here at Ravenport, or was this all for her and the Earl?

Emily saw the footmen's attention wander to the door before she heard anyone behind her, and she turned, following the direction of their eyes.

"Oh," she said in surprise. "Good morning."

The little girl simply stared back at her. She had dark hair and blue-green eyes that seemed rather familiar, though Emily wasn't entirely sure why that would be so. The child, who Emily placed as younger than ten, took steps into the room, picking up a plate as she began to serve herself.

"Are you here to visit for Christmas?" Emily asked, looking past the girl in search of a parent or a governess, but she seemed to be alone — and still did not respond to her questions. "Ah, a berry scone. Those are my favorite as well. Tell me, which cheese do you prefer? There are so many, I cannot seem to choose, and my plate isn't big enough for all of them."

The little girl tentatively reached out a finger and pointed to the Swiss, which Emily selected and placed upon her plate.

"Excellent choice," she said, "that looks divine."

The girl looked up at her with the slightest smile on her face, which Emily answered with one of her own.

"Now," Emily said, turning to look at the long chestnut dining room table, set for twelve places. "Where am I to sit?"

The girl held her plate in one hand and surprised Emily by taking her other hand within hers, leading her over to a place one down from the head of the table. She pointed Emily to the chair and took the one next to her before she began to eat.

"It's nice to meet you," Emily continued as she picked up her fork and knife. "I am Mrs. Nicholls. And you?"

The girl looked over at her out of the corner of her eye, before finally saying in a voice just above a whisper, "Margaret."

"Margaret! What a beautiful name," Emily gushed. "Does anyone ever call you Peggy?"

She shook her head, her face impassive. "No."

"Margaret it is then."

The girl nodded.

"What do you think of Ravenport Hall?" Emily asked, bringing a forkful of egg to her mouth, hopeful that she might somehow ease the girl's stoic resolve. "It is rather fine, is it not?"

"I suppose," Margaret said, lifting her fork tentatively.

"Do you have a favorite room?" Emily continued, keeping her voice light. She didn't want to annoy the child, but she hoped she would begin to open up to her. Was she always this quiet, Emily wondered, or was she simply as intimidated as Emily was by this estate and its opulence?

"The music room," Margaret responded, true joy alighting her face, and Emily smiled. This was something upon which they could find common ground. She wouldn't say she was overly talented, but she did enjoy playing the pianoforte and singing along when she had the chance.

"I haven't yet seen that room," Emily said warmly. "Perhaps you could show me later on. Would you play for me?"

Margaret nodded much more enthusiastically now, and then, to Emily's surprise, began to tell her all about the piece she was currently attempting to master. Emily listened attentively while she continued to eat her breakfast until she heard the tread of a heavy foot behind them.

"Margaret?" came the voice, one Emily recognized. When she turned, she saw with a jolt that Margaret's aquamarine eyes were staring back at her, but from a different face — that of the Earl.

He must be her father.

6

His daughter was speaking. Animatedly.

Charles had stood in shock for a moment upon entering the dining room. Who was this girl, chattering on about some song or another in such great detail?

He remembered the night he first met Mrs. Nicholls and the scene he had witnessed between her and the Coningsby children. She clearly enjoyed young ones, as evident by her profession, and obviously, his daughter had responded.

Charles didn't want to admit the pang of pain that raced through him upon the fact that she refused to say even a word to him.

So much for his deliberations as to how to best introduce Mrs. Nicholls to his daughter. It seemed that it had all happened regardless of his intentions.

"Margaret?" he repeated as the two women now stared at him from their places next to one another at the table. Somehow, he felt the outsider, despite the fact that sitting in front of him in his own dining room was his daughter and his betrothed — well, for a time, at least.

"Lord Doverton," Mrs. Nicholls exclaimed, rising from the table with a small curtsy. "Good morning."

His daughter surprised him by following suit.

"I was incredibly lucky to have found myself such a lovely companion for breakfast," Mrs. Nicholls said with a smile at the girl. "Margaret must be your daughter."

The girl in question stared blankly back at him, as Charles nodded.

"She is."

"Well, she is quite lovely, Lord Doverton. I can hardly believe you have kept her such a secret."

Her tone was light but her eyes were accusatory. While Charles felt the need to defend himself, he could hardly blame her for being upset that he would keep such information from her. He wasn't entirely sure how to explain himself. The topic of Margaret simply... hadn't come up He cleared his throat as he determined what to say, but Mrs. Nicholls continued on, saving him.

"Margaret is going to show me her music room this morning when we are finished breakfast," she said. "Perhaps you would like to join us?"

"I, ah... I'm not entirely sure—" he said, his eyes on his daughter to gauge her reaction, but she remained as stoic as ever, not saying a word.

"We will begin and will wait for you to join us," Mrs. Nicholls said with a pointed look, and suddenly Charles became well aware of what it would be like to be under her care as a governess. "We shall see you shortly. Come, Margaret, please show me the way. I believe I require a map in order to find my way around this estate. This *beautiful* estate," she added, entirely for his benefit, he was sure.

And so it was sometime later that Charles found himself walking through the great hall, the saloon, and finally, the library before he took the curved corridor to the music room.

Until several weeks ago when he had found his daughter there, it had been years since Charles had seen the music room, and now here he was, visiting it once more for the second time in a month. This wing of the house had been built solely for Miriam's pleasure. She had enjoyed music, but even more so, she'd enjoyed spending his money on various renovations and additions to his estate.

But Margaret seemed quite taken with the room, so in the end, he supposed, it was worth it.

The walls were cream, one of the few rooms in the estate that wasn't adorned with wallpaper. Between sconces hung on the wall were a wide array of landscape paintings. Seeing Margaret and Mrs. Nicholls seated next to one another on the bench in front of the pianoforte, he took a seat in one of the blue upholstered sofas that were pushed against the walls on the outskirts of the room.

"Now," Mrs. Nicholls said as she bent her blond head closer to Margaret's dark one. "This one is called 'Deck the Halls.'"

"'Deck the Halls'?"

"Yes. It's all about preparing the manor for Christmas."

"But the servants do that. And not until it is the day before Christmas."

"Well, then aren't we lucky that tomorrow is Christmas Eve?"

"Is it?"

"Of course!" Mrs. Nicholls exclaimed. "Have you... have you a governess, Margaret?"

"Not anymore."

"Oh?" Mrs. Nicholls said, and Charles was about to rise, angry that she would think to question the girl so, for this had nothing to do with her. He stopped, however, as he realized he was more interested in hearing the remainder of the conversation.

"Miss Kedleston left a week before Father arrived home." The girl paused for a moment before adding in a voice so soft he had to strain to hear her words, "She said I was most difficult."

"You? Difficult?" Mrs. Nicholls said, astonishment in her voice and on her face. "I can hardly imagine that to be the case."

In fact, Miss Kedleston had written and said it was difficult to teach a pupil who would not say a word to her. Apparently, Margaret punished anyone she didn't like with silence. Charles had understood, despairing of what he was supposed to do with his daughter. She had always been here, at Ravenport with Miriam. He had tried to visit, had attempted to be part of her life, but Miriam was clear that she had no wish for him to live here. He could have forced the issue, but it was easier to leave her be. Miriam had, however, filled her daughter's head with lies about him, and the girl had never seen him as anything but the enemy.

Then Miriam was gone, leaving Margaret, who believed her father to be a cold monster who wanted nothing to do with her. Which was so far from the truth.

"I bet your Miss Kedleston simply didn't know how to work with someone as intelligent as you," Mrs. Nicholls said with a smile for the girl, and it warmed Charles' heart to see his daughter smile in return, even if her expression was directed at someone else. "Now, let me teach you this song."

She began picking out the notes, singing along with them as she went. She had a lovely voice, one that could certainly hold a melody and was enjoyable to listen to. Her face lit radiantly as the tune filled the room, and his throat thickened with emotion. In fact, Charles was so taken with her, sitting there, playing with a smile on her face, that he received a jolt when he heard his daughter speak once more.

"I think I have the tune now."

"You do?" Mrs. Nicholls asked, and Charles was as surprised as she. But whereas he would insist on continuing to instruct the girl, Mrs. Nicholls urged her to play. And so she did. Charles had heard Margaret play once before, but he could hardly believe how masterfully she had learned the song in just moments. The girl had talent, that was for certain. Mrs. Nicholls began singing along with the girl's playing, and after a moment, Margaret joined in, her voice soft and high.

"Deck the halls with boughs of holly, fa-la-la-la, la-la-la-la;
'Tis the season to be jolly, fa-la-la-la, la-la-la-la...."

As Charles listened to the pair of them, a strange, joyous warmth began to creep through his chest. He listened to the words of the song, which painted a picture of seasonal festivities and gaiety. To him, Christmas had always been a religious occasion accompanied by a fine meal, family he would prefer not to visit with, and a celebration at the end of it all. Not this all-encompassing festive season, which, he must admit, sounded rather enjoyable.

They finished on a resounding, "Fa-la-la-la, la-la-la-la," before the two of them broke into laughter. Charles slowly clapped his hands as he stood and approached them.

"Very well done," he said, and his daughter instantly dropped her eyes, though Mrs. Nicholls smiled at him — a very becoming smile, as it were. Now that they were closer, he could see that tiny freckles dotted her slim nose, upon which her spectacles perched. Behind them, her eyes were the color of sherry, and they seemed to see right through him to his very soul — one he tried rather hard to hide from others. Life, as an earl, was not one that was to be filled with joy and emotion and warm Christmas tidings. It was a life of doing one's duty, such as hosting family he would rather remain in their own homes.

"Thank you, Lord Doverton," Mrs. Nicholls said, and he nodded.

"It might be best for you to call me Charles," he reminded her, and she paled but nodded.

"Thank you for entertaining my friend, Margaret," he said gently. "I would like to show her some of the other rooms of the house if you would care to accompany us?"

She shook her head and returned to the pianoforte. "I will play awhile," she said, and Charles decided he would take that as a win, for she had, at the very least, used words to answer him.

"Mrs. Nicholls— Emily..." He looked to her for approval to use her name, and continued when she nodded. "Would you care to join me for a tour of the estate?"

"Very well," she said, standing and then turning back to Margaret. "Shall we meet up for luncheon, Margaret?"

The girl nodded, and Charles held out his arm. Emily looked at it for a moment, slightly unsure, but then slipped her hand through his arm and upon it. Charles took the opportunity to review her dress. It fit her to near perfection, and she actually looked rather lovely draped in cream muslin. The modiste had done her job well.

"You should likely have an idea of how to find your way around before the guests arrive," he said as he led her out of the music room. He noted how delicate her bare fingers were upon his arm. It had been some time since he had escorted a woman.

"I feel as though you could show me the rooms dozens of times and I still wouldn't be able to find my way," she said with a bit of a laugh, and when he looked over at her, he noted the dimple in the corner of her cheek that appeared when she smiled.

"I realize the estate is somewhat extravagant," he admitted. "But it is the family manor, and I am used to it. When you spend days as a boy playing hide-and-seek behind the columns of the marble hall, somehow they don't seem quite as foreboding."

She smiled at his story. Despite himself, he found her easy to talk to. "Have you siblings? Will they be joining us?"

He tried not to frown at her words. "I do not. My mother died in childbirth, and my father never remarried. I have cousins, however."

"Such as the one I met at the Coninsbys' ball?"

"Yes, unfortunately. Edward can be rather... indelicate, I suppose you could say."

"And the rest of your cousins?" she asked as he led her through the saloon, pausing with her as she stopped to look up at the rosettes and octagonal compartments on the domed ceiling.

"Most fall into the same vein as Edward," he mused, "though there are some whose company I enjoy. I'm afraid that my grandfather pitted my father and his brother against one another their entire lives — he felt competition was a method to betterment — which has continued on through the rest of the family."

She looked up at him with pity on her face. Pity that he had no time for. "I am sorry to hear it."

"It is part of this life, Mrs. Nicholls, one in which you are blessedly only joining for a couple of weeks."

They began walking again, circling back through the hall to the drawing room. There, he took a seat on one of the uncomfortable pink chairs and gestured for her to take another.

"Have you any questions of me, Emily?" he asked, hoping she would be satisfied with what she had already encountered and ask no more of him. He had some ledgers to review this morning. There was much work to be done before the madness that would come along with his family, who would arrive tomorrow.

"Just one," she said, looking up at him with wide eyes full of a mix of trepidation and curiosity. "Why is your daughter so afraid of you?"

7

Emily knew that Lord Doverton wouldn't be pleased with her question. But if she was going to spend any amount of time with the man, however brief and contrived it might be, she had to know the answer. She refused to be betrothed — even falsely betrothed — to a man who ill-treated his child.

"Pardon me?" he said, biting the words out, his stoic countenance breaking as he flinched back in defense. "Margaret is not *frightened* of me."

"No?" Emily said, her mouth drying, yet she pressed on nonetheless. "Then why will she hardly speak a word in your presence? Why does she practically cower when you enter the room?"

Lord Doverton — Charles, she reminded herself — sighed as he stood, running a hand through his dark hair. For a moment, Emily thought he looked rather desperate, his neck stiff, his forearms strained, though she couldn't be entirely certain as when he dropped his hand, the look was gone once more and the stoic lord had returned.

He walked over to the hearth, staring down at it before turning back to her.

"As you may have gathered, I was married — to Margaret's mother."

Emily nodded, hoping with her silence that he would continue. He did.

"Being my father's only son — his only *child* — he pressured me to marry early, to begin to produce heirs so that the family line would continue should something ever happen to me. Miriam was from a good family. She showed interest in me, she was beautiful, and she came from a family of six. Her sister already had three children before she was five-and-twenty. My father considered her a good bet to produce children, and who was I to argue?"

Emily bit her lip. It hardly seemed to her to be a reason to marry, but then, no one had asked for her opinion.

"We got along fine, at first. We were civil to one another, enjoyed many of the same social outings, had common acquaintances, though we weren't overly friendly, I suppose you could say." He paused for a moment, looking rather uncomfortable. "After six years together, Miriam still had not given birth to any children."

"I see," Emily said, her gut wrenching for the woman, understanding her plight.

"By this point in time, we were not getting on well. She had little time for me. I believe she required more attention from me, but I had responsibilities as well. She then became so bitter that it was difficult to spend any amount of time with her. She thought herself a failure. While I wished for children, I was not so stupid a man as to put the blame on her. It was not as though she had done anything wrong."

That was more than most men would have assumed, and for that, Emily gave him some credit.

"Finally she became pregnant, though she didn't tell me until she was well into her fifth month. I was living in London by then, you see, and she remained here. Miriam had invested all her time into renovating the Hall. We visited one another now and again, but we primarily lived apart."

"That is rather sad," Emily murmured, and Charles shrugged.

"It is the way of it among many."

Many in the nobility, perhaps. Emily could hardly imagine anyone she knew having two homes to retreat to. Her parents had blessedly been happy, although she had seen many who lived their lives together in misery. Although she supposed that, at the very least, her parents had had the option to choose one another, unlike many of Charles' class.

"Then she had Margaret. She considered herself a failure once more for having a daughter instead of a son. But that baby..." he looked over Emily's head now, his gaze directed beyond the window, although his mind was elsewhere. "She was the most beautiful thing I had ever seen."

"That's lovely," Emily said encouragingly, as there was clearly more to this story.

Lord Doverton cleared his throat.

"Yes, well, Miriam basically banished me. She wanted nothing more to do with me. Didn't want to try for another baby as she said it would only bring about far too much disappointment. I could have stayed if I had chosen, of course, but it seemed best to provide her with the space she desired."

He looked down, his fingers tightening on the back of the chair he leaned against. "It was a mistake. Miriam filled Margaret's head with all sorts of lies about me so that

Margaret wanted nothing to do with me, desired me gone to the same extent her mother did. Then Miriam died of consumption, and her plan caused her only child to lose both parents. Margaret believes I am a terrible man. That I hurt her mother, that I wanted nothing to do with her. That I left her because I *chose* to leave her." He shut his eyes tightly. "That is not the case, and yet I do not see how I can convince her otherwise."

Emily's heart reached out toward the man who was now showing her more emotion than he likely had ever shown another before. Here was a man who was suffering, struggling. He may seem rather cold, but Emily had a feeling that the front he wore was in order to protect himself and the emotions within.

"Well," she said optimistically, "the good news is that you now have the opportunity to put things right. Show Margaret the man you really are and how you truly feel about her."

"It's too late," he said, straightening, reining in whatever emotion he had allowed for a moment.

"It is never too late."

"I thank you for your positivity, Emily, but it is," he said, his words clipped. "Now, I'd best retire to the study for a time as there is much to do."

Emily looked up at him in disconcert.

"But it's Christmas Eve tomorrow!"

"Exactly," he said, his brow furrowed, clearly not understanding her protestation. "The family will arrive tomorrow late in the day, so I'd best complete all I need to today."

"We should begin preparations for Christmas," Emily said, rising as well. "I'm sure Margaret would love to do so, and she would enjoy it even more if you were there as well."

"Please, Emily," Charles said, holding up a hand, "do not

force the issue. The relationship between my daughter and me is our own. I informed you of it so that you were aware, but there are no further actions that you must take."

"But—"

"I mean it, Emily."

Emily nodded, but she didn't agree to anything. The little girl deserved a father, and there was a perfectly good one standing right here, even if he didn't know it yet. He might not know how to express it, but he clearly loved his daughter, and that was all she needed to know.

"Very well," she said. "I am going to go speak to Toller."

"My butler?" he asked, looking rather surprised.

"Yes, your butler," she said. "Do you know another Toller?"

He opened his mouth, and Emily cringed, afraid she had gone rather too far, but she forged on anyway.

"I must tell him that if the servants have not already selected a Yule Log, I would like to arrange to do so myself tomorrow."

"Whatever for?" he said, rather perplexed.

"Because I enjoy doing such a thing, Charles," she said. "In fact, I enjoy most activities that surround Christmas."

"But Christmas is—"

"A religious holiday, yes, I understand," she said, running her hands over the fabric of her beautiful new morning dress. "But I believe it is also a time for giving of oneself, and of enjoying all that we have to be grateful for. And you, Lord Doverton, have much to be thankful for in your life."

"Charles," he corrected her. "And yes, I realize that. I know my estate is more than most have—"

"It is not your home to which I refer," she corrected him, though he clearly had no idea what she meant by that.

"Should you care to join me, I will go tomorrow afternoon. First, however, I would like to do some baking with Margaret."

"Baking?" he repeated, "but we have cooks to do that."

"Oh, Charles," she said, smiling at him and how little he understood about who she was or what Christmas was about. "I hope someday you come to feel the way I do."

And with that, she left him there with his hands in his hair once more.

WHAT HAD he gotten himself into?

Charles had imagined that if he had to pretend to be betrothed to someone, a governess would be a good bet. No one would know who she was, and therefore, when they went their separate ways, there would be no ramifications. Besides that, she would be demure, following his lead, doing as he said, not questioning any decisions or issues within their relationship for the time that they would be together.

He was beginning to realize just how wrong he was.

Who was this Mrs. Nicholls? On the surface, she certainly *looked* the part of governess, with her simple chignon, her spectacles, and the plain dresses she had worn until he'd presented her with a new wardrobe.

But after a few conversations, he was finding that underneath the exterior package was someone else entirely.

First of all, she had this strange fascination with Christmas. Why, he had no idea. Then there were her views on his family, which she had no business questioning. He had explained his relationship with his daughter, providing her with far more information than he had intended, but he had no need for her to improve it. It was too late to save it. After this Christmas was over, he would find a bride that would suit who would look after Margaret, he would beget an heir, and he would have this whole business with Edward over and done with.

He just had to get through the next few days.

Charles meandered into his study, which was one room that Miriam hadn't touched. It was ironic, however, for it was the one room that he would have liked to have changed, as it reminded him so much of his father. His father, who had always been so cold, so calculating, so unable to show Charles even a modicum of affection.

He shifted uncomfortably as he took a seat in the desk chair and Emily's words came back to him regarding his own daughter. Was he becoming the same man his father had been? Except that in this case, it was not his fault that there was such a chasm between them — it was the fault of his wife, who had turned the girl against him.

He had just opened one of his ledgers and was beginning to review expenses when the housekeeper knocked and hurried into the room.

"My lord?" his housekeeper inquired urgently. While Toller had always been loyal to him and his family, Miriam had hired Mrs. Graydon. Although she had always maintained a polite reserve, he could sense that she was as turned against him as Margaret.

"Yes, Mrs. Graydon?" he asked, attempting patience, as the housekeeper wrung her hands together.

"It's just that... Mrs. Nicholls, she's in the kitchens."

"Oh yes," he said, waving a hand in the air. "I believe she was going to do some baking."

"Well, Cook is *quite* agitated. You see, she had already planned all of the desserts and pastries to accompany the Christmas meal, and now Mrs. Nicholls is adding something else. Cook also doesn't want to insult her, but what if what she makes is hardly edible? How do we not serve them to your family without insulting Mrs. Nicholls?"

Charles sighed.

"I'm certain this is not a matter that requires my attention, Mrs. Graydon."

"Toller said the same thing," said the woman. "But without a lady of the house, I know not where else to turn as Mrs. Nicholls does not seem inclined to listen to me, and I cannot very well tell her what to do."

"No, Mrs. Graydon, you cannot."

Emily Nicholls might not be in actuality his intended, but to his staff she was.

"I will speak to her, but Mrs. Graydon, Mrs. Nicholls will be treated as the lady of the manor. Do you understand?"

Mrs. Graydon colored but nodded her head as Charles rose to see what exactly was occurring in his kitchens.

8

I t had been some time since Charles had entered into the kitchens of Ravenport Hall. As a young boy, he had spent much time down here, stealing pies and pastries after dinner, especially if his father had sent him to bed without. But since he had become the lord of the manor, he had felt that it was rather beneath him to occupy this wing of the house, which included the kitchens and all of the servants' quarters.

"Now, Margaret," he could hear Emily's voice from within as he strode down the corridor, "it's important to mix the wet ingredients in one bowl and the dry in another. Then we will mix them all together afterward, all right?"

"Yes, Mrs. Nicholls," she said obediently.

"Have you ever baked pastries before?"

"No, I haven't."

"Well, you're in luck. This is my mother's recipe."

Charles poked his head in the door to see Emily and Margaret bent over mixing bowls at the end of the counter, all manner of ingredients in front of them. The cook was going about her business, although every now and then she would glance over at the pair at the opposite end. Her gaze, however, was not hostile as the housekeeper had suggested, but rather interested in all that was happening.

The cook spotted Charles before anyone else did, and when she looked up at him, he held a finger to his lips so that she wouldn't say anything. He'd prefer to observe his daughter before she realized he was in the room, as then she was more than likely to retreat back into the shell she seemed to inhabit whenever she was in his presence.

"What comes first?" she asked, and Emily began reading the ingredients off the list, having the girl organize them in front of her as she did so.

They measured and poured, beat and mixed as Charles watched. Their backs were primarily toward him and therefore he stayed out of their line of sight. It was certainly not the scene he had expected when he came down here after Mrs. Graydon's complaint, but it seemed it was she who had the issue and not so much the cook.

With a cup of flour clutched in her hand, Emily glanced at Margaret and held it out. "Would you like to pour this in?"

Charles finally walked into the room and sauntered over toward them. "What are you making?"

Emily let out an alarmed yelp as she whipped around toward him. As she did so, the cup of flour jerked, the contents of it flying out toward him, covering him in white powder.

Charles stood still for a moment before raising his hands to wipe the flour from his eyes.

"Well, perhaps this is why I never venture down to the kitchens," he said, as he looked down at his buff breeches, green waistcoat and black jacket, now covered in a fine dusting of flour. When he raised his eyes, they met Emily's.

Hers were as wide as could be, her hand clutching her chest as she stared at him.

"Lord Doverton — ah, that is Charles — I am incredibly sorry. I didn't hear you enter and it's just, well, you startled me."

"My apologies," he said curtly, though he wasn't entirely sure if the hastiness of her actions was warranted. "I shouldn't have come. I had thought—"

He stopped abruptly, however, when he saw the look on his daughter's face. If he wasn't mistaken, that was a... *smile* he saw there. He couldn't recall the last time he had seen an expression of joy on her face. Well, if that made her laugh...

He reached down, brushing some of the flour off of his jacket and into his hand.

"I suppose, Emily, there is only one thing to do about it."

"Wh-what's that?" she asked, standing a step back toward the counter as though putting some distance between them might protect her.

He leaned in, stretching out his hand toward her. Before she could react, he had cupped her face in his hand and smeared the flour over her cheek and nose.

"There," he said with a grin. "Much better. We match now."

Emily's mouth opened into a round 'O' before she started to laugh as she rubbed the flour from her nose.

"Why, Charles, I didn't know you had it in you!"

He looked over to Margaret, and her initial smile had widened into more of a grin.

"Margaret!" he said, trying not to allow the hurt to invade when he saw that her smile faded somewhat when he said her name. "There is something wrong with your face."

ELLIE ST. CLAIR

"My face?" she said, biting her lip now as it trembled slightly at his words.

"Why yes," he said contemplatively. "It is a bit too... clean."

And with that, he placed an ever-so-light dusting of flour on top her nose.

"Father!" she said with some shock, and now it was his turn to smile wide. It was the first time he could remember her calling him as such. Or addressing him at all.

"If flour is so much to your liking, Charles," Emily said innocently, "then you really must try some of the chocolate sauce."

She took a spoon from the bowl of wet ingredients and held it out toward him. He eyed her suspiciously, but she seemed to be making amends. When he went to take a bite off the spoon, however, she pulled it back away from him and smeared it on his chin before she finally let him taste it. It was... decadent. He wiped his chin with his finger and then held it out to her.

"Have you tried any, Emily?"

"I have not," she said, pulling her head back. "I shall wait until we finish."

"That's no fun," he said, raising one eyebrow, and then placed his finger on her nose instead. She gave out a cry, and soon enough the three of them were flinging all sorts of ingredients back and forth. There was sugar in their hair, flour on the floor, and molasses covering the countertop.

Somehow, in the melee, Charles' finger, still covered in chocolate, came to rest on Emily's lips. He removed it quickly, but then watched as she slowly licked the chocolate off her lips. It did something to him, causing his breeches to tighten as he thought of what else she might do with that pink tongue.

He shook his head immediately to clear the unbidden thought. What in heaven's name was he thinking? He was an earl for goodness sake, one who had no time for such thoughts regarding the governess who was supposed to be nothing more than a placeholder until he had time to find a true bride.

"What is going on in here?"

They all froze as still as statues at the reprimand from the doorway before they turned as one to find Mrs. Graydon standing there staring at all of them. "The kitchen is destroyed!"

"I am sorry, Mrs. Graydon," Emily said shamefully. "We became rather... carried away."

"Carried away!" she exclaimed. "Why this is... this is..."

"This is my kitchen," Charles said, turning to her now, his voice of authority back. The scolding from the housekeeper was a reminder of his place — and hers. He had been so caught up in trying to appease his daughter — and Emily, if he were being honest — that he had forgotten just who he was and all he was responsible for in front of his servants. They would lose all respect for him. He should never have been playing around with food, let alone be present in the kitchens of his manor.

"While I agree that this mess is rather untoward, I also pay all of you to clean it, do I not?"

"Yes, my lord, you do," Mrs. Graydon said, though her eyes didn't convey the same sincerity as her words.

"We will help clean up the mess," Emily said quickly, but then Charles turned his gaze on her.

"No, you will not," he said, holding up a finger to emphasize how serious his order was. "Mrs. Graydon is aware that you are to be treated as the lady of this house at the moment."

Recognition dawned in Emily's eyes, as she clearly caught the significance of his last words, "at the moment." Until such time came that she would return to Lord and Lady Coningsby's in her role as governess — a far cry from lady of the house. Damn but this whole charade was becoming rather ridiculous. This was why he typically kept everything so aboveboard. One falsehood only led to another until one was so deep that he was unsure of just which way to turn.

"Thank you, Mrs. Graydon," he said to the steely eyed woman at the door. "That will be all. Now," he said, returning to Emily and Margaret, who stood looking down as though they were chastised schoolgirls. He softened his tone. "The two of you can continue on with what you were baking before I interrupted. I look forward to tasting it."

"Thank you, Charles," Emily said quietly as she handed Margaret a cloth before finding one for herself. She removed her spectacles to wipe her face, and when she did, he caught a much better glimpse of her warm brown eyes than he ever had before. For a moment, he thought he could drown in their sherry depths, forgetting everything else he was supposed to do, was responsible for, and just stare at her.

Then she returned the spectacles to her nose and dipped her head to review the recipe below her, and the moment was gone, though he couldn't help it from burning into his memory.

He cleared his throat.

"I will just... ah... leave you to it, then," he said, and then he turned on his heel and retreated as fast as he could before either of these females caused him to lose all rational thought once more.

9

Emily knocked on the door of the earl's study, as hesitant now as she had been when she had knocked on the door of this manor. She looked down at the plate in her hands, filled now with the cinnamon scones that she and Margaret had finally been successful in creating, among other pastries, with a bit of help from the cook.

He had said he had wanted to try them, and in a way, she felt the need to apologize for the disaster in the kitchen today. Although, perhaps, it was not *entirely* unfortunate, for Margaret had seemed quite enthralled by the situation.

She had talked about it for quite some time following her father's departure. "—and did you *see* him, covered in flour?" she had exclaimed with a giggle, which Emily had answered with one of her own. She had to admit that it had been quite a sight, the Earl of Doverton standing there in his formerly immaculate clothing, completely covered in white flour with chocolate all over his face.

Until Mrs. Graydon had arrived. Emily did not exactly receive warm feelings from the woman, and she had a notion that she would be quite relieved upon Emily's departure — which was in a short two weeks, she reminded herself.

The door suddenly opened and she jumped slightly as the earl stood there awaiting her.

"My, but you startle easily," the earl said as he opened the door wider to allow her entrance.

"I do," she admitted. "I confess, it is not one of my finer points."

"Well, if that is the worst of your habits, I do not think you have much to be concerned about."

"That is kind of you to say, my lord."

"Charles."

"Yes, Charles," she said, biting her lip. "My apologies. It is difficult to become accustomed to calling you such after spending so many years as a governess."

"At least that has provided you with knowledge on the workings of such an estate as this," he said as he waved a hand toward the leather chesterfield and chair that surrounded a mahogany table. It matched his monstrous desk against one side of the wall.

"It does, it's true," she said. "Though I am becoming rather nervous about your family's arrival."

"Never fear them," he said, seemingly without worry. "Just be polite and stay out of their way."

Well, wasn't that reassurance to assuage her fears, Emily thought as Charles took a seat on the chair while she perched on the corner of the chesterfield.

"Oh, I've brought you some scones," she said, holding them out toward him. "They are cinnamon."

He didn't hesitate to reach out and take one from her.

"I shouldn't have one before dinner," he said, ever disciplined, "but I've never been able to help myself when it comes to something sweet."

He took a bite, his eyes widening. "Well, Emily," he said when he had finished his mouthful. "You're a woman of many talents. You certainly can bake."

Her cheeks warmed. "My mother taught me," she said.

He looked down at the pastry he held in his hands.

"I must apologize, for taking you from your family this Christmas," he said quietly before raising his eyes to hers. "It seems you must be quite close."

"We are," she said with a sad smile. "My father is not well, unfortunately. His lungs are failing."

"I'm sorry to hear that," he said, his brow creasing. "Is there anything to be done?"

"I do not think so," she said, "at least not according to our village physician."

"Your parents are not far," he said, a thoughtful look on his face. "Once Christmas is over, I shall send my own physician from London to see to him."

Emily shook her head fiercely at his words.

"Oh, no, my lo— Charles. I couldn't ask you to do that."

"Why ever not?"

"The cost would likely be far too high," she said without shame. "With what you have given us, I know it would likely cover much of it, but I was planning to use that to keep him comfortable and to hire someone to check in on my parents and help look after them while my sister and I work. Your physician, while I'm sure he is quite competent, would likely be an unnecessary expense."

"I would pay for it," he said, leaning forward toward her.

Emily longed to say yes, thank you, for she would do anything for her father. But she couldn't ask Charles for more. He had already been more than generous.

"I can't—"

"You will," he said, settling back in his chair once more.

"Do you always just do as you please, despite what anyone else has to say about it?" she asked, raising an eyebrow as well as one corner of her lips so that he would realize she was partially jesting.

"Usually," he said with a shrug. "That is one of the aspects of being an earl that I enjoy most."

She nodded as he looked at her shrewdly.

"Let me guess — you helped clean the kitchen today, didn't you?"

She opened her mouth to deny his words, but couldn't keep herself from providing the truth.

"I did," she said with a grimace. She knew he would be disappointed, for he was so adamant that she not do so, but she hadn't been able to help herself, despite his command to the contrary. "I did, after all, make the mess," she said in defense. "And besides, Cook and the scullery maids already had much to do, with tomorrow being Christmas Eve already."

He slightly smiled but shook his head at her. "Ah, Emily, you may know the workings of a household such as this, but you have much to learn about becoming a countess."

She raised an eyebrow. "Then it's best, perhaps, that I will not in actuality be doing so."

They were both silent for a moment at her words and Emily instantly regretted them. It had seemed as though they were coming to a place of friendship if nothing else, and now she had ruined the moment.

He took another bite of the scone, and Emily stood, unsure of what else there was to say.

"I'd best be going," she said, running her hands down her skirts, which were now a deep purple, for she had changed following the chaos in the kitchen. Strangely, she didn't want to leave. She felt drawn to be here, with him, despite the fact that she knew they were worlds away from one another.

He nodded in agreement, however, and so she knew it was time to go, as she had realized he expected everyone to follow along with his wishes — and rightly so. It was his house, after all.

She had just placed her hand on the doorknob when he called out.

"Emily?"

She turned.

"Do you know how to dance?"

"Somewhat," she said, biting her lip, although her heart beat fast at the thought of actually putting into practice what she knew in front of a room full of people. "There are some dances I learned as a child, and others I have witnessed my charges learn. I have practiced with them."

"Have you ever danced the waltz — with a man?"

Emily swallowed hard.

"I have not."

"Well, then," he said. "We dance some evenings, and there will be a ball here on Twelfth Night. You will need to know the steps. After dinner, meet me in the saloon and we shall ensure you know exactly what to do."

"Oh, Charles, I don't think—"

"Please, Emily," he said calmly, and she nodded quickly. He had put it as a question, but it was clearly more than that.

"Very well."

And then she hurried out the door so that he couldn't see the fear that she knew would be upon her face.

For it was not the dancing that she dreaded. No, she

worried that she would like dancing with Charles far more than she should, which would never do at all.

～

EMILY HEARD the strains of music before she even set foot in the saloon. It was tinny, chiming, and not a tune she recognized.

She had fretted about this dance all through dinner, which had been somewhat quiet and rather tense. She had attempted to make conversation but had nearly given up with exhaustion after doing all she could to ease the strain between father and daughter, who hardly spoke aside from commenting on the dishes in front of them.

Meanwhile, she had been searching her brain for a reason as to why she couldn't meet the earl tonight to dance with him, but she knew he would see through any excuse she attempted.

And so, here she was, standing outside the saloon door, where she was going to dance with an earl.

She chuckled under her breath as she thought of her family and what they would say if she told them this was her current situation. James would have laughed at the absurdity of it all. No one would ever believe her. And why would they? She could hardly believe it herself. She wouldn't if it wasn't for the tangible evidence of the man awaiting her. It was something like a fairy tale, really, except in this, there was no happily-ever-after.

So Emily couldn't have been more surprised when she opened the door to find the earl standing in the middle of the saloon, his brow furrowed in concentration as he held an imaginary partner in his arms, his mouth moving as he counted the steps while circling the room.

He had excellent timing, she would give him that, she thought, tilting her head as though critiquing one of the children she looked after. However, he needed some additional work on his decorum, for he seemed a little too stiff...

"Emily!" he exclaimed as he turned in her direction, immediately stopping and placing his arms behind his back as though he could hide what he had been doing. "My apologies, I didn't hear you come in."

"There is no need to apologize," she said, biting her cheek to keep from grinning. "I see you are practicing. I would have thought you would be well-versed in the waltz."

She thought it rather endearing when his cheeks turned bright red.

"Yes, well, it is a relatively new dance, and I cannot say I have made it a habit to partake much."

"I see," she said, though she didn't at all. If he wanted a wife so badly then why was he not wooing a woman who would be far more suitable than she?

"Well," she said instead, quite diplomatically, "I am not a complete novice, so perhaps an actual partner might be of some use to you."

"Very well," he said.

He walked over to the side of the room, stopping at a small side table. Curious, Emily followed him over.

"Is that a music box?"

She had heard of them, though she hadn't seen one before.

"It is," he said, beginning to wind it. "It was my mother's. I believe her father bought it for her in Germany. I have a small collection of a few mementos of hers — this, a hairbrush, and a couple of pieces of jewelry."

Emily could hardly fathom having only a few items to

remember her mother by. She had more trinkets of her mother's in her carrying case alone.

"The music, conveniently, is in three-quarter time, so amenable to a waltz. My apologies, but we'll have just the one song."

"One song is all we need," she said with an encouraging smile.

He held out his hand to her, and Emily nearly jumped when she took it, so much was the shock of his warm hand upon hers. She wasn't wearing gloves, for having never had many occasions to wear them before, they certainly didn't feel comfortable here when she was around the house.

He turned her so that they were facing one another, their hands clasped, and then when he put his free hand on her waist, she tentatively lifted her other hand to his shoulder. Their eyes met, and she attempted to slow her breathing at their proximity. The scent of his cologne, a spicy sage, filled her, causing a heady swoon for a moment.

She tried to ignore just how handsome he was. How strong his currently rather-clenched jaw was, how blue his eyes were, even though they seemed rather hard and just the slightest bit icy.

Emily closed her eyes for just a moment as she tried to dissuade any fanciful thoughts from entering her mind. This was a man who had basically hired her to parade as his future wife for two weeks and then leave his life forever. She would return to her role as a governess. She'd best not forget it.

"Is everything all right, Emily?"

Emily. The sound of her name on his lips was almost too much to bear as she was trying to convince herself that she could never develop feelings for this most uncaring man. This was her opportunity to create an excuse of feeling ill, to run from this room and not return until she was back in a rational state of mind.

"I'm fine," came out of her mouth instead, and she sighed inwardly.

"How did you manage to escape your latest charge?" he questioned, and she had to ask him to repeat himself, for she couldn't tear her eyes away from his lips as he spoke.

"My charge?" she repeated.

"My daughter," he said slowly. "You seem to have adopted her as your latest work. You are not a governess here, you know."

"Of course not," she said, his words snapping her out of whatever idea she might have had about him. "I *choose* to spend time with her. She is quite lovely."

"I imagine she is," he said with a sigh. "I must make a confession."

"Very well."

She was certainly curious as to what this might be.

"I envy you."

"Me?" she squeaked.

"Yes," he said, nodding. "You have come to know my daughter better in one day than I have in eight years. I only wish that she would allow me to become closer to her."

"Have you ever thought to tell her the truth?"

"No," he shook his head. "She loved her mother. Now that she is gone... I would not want to tarnish the memory of her. Besides that, Margaret likely wouldn't believe me, and it would seem that I am only attempting to turn the girl against her mother who is no longer able to defend herself."

Emily's estimation of the man grew slightly.

"That is honorable of you."

"I don't believe honor is the right word. Honor would have been staying when it was difficult. Making peace with

Miriam in order to be with my daughter. Not running when all became difficult."

"All is not lost," Emily said, squeezing his shoulder urgently before she even realized what she was doing. "You are still able to repair the relationship."

"I will try," he said, and then looked intently at her. "Will you help me?"

Emily was startled for a moment but then nodded slowly as a smile began to form on her lips.

"That, Charles, I will gladly do."

As they twirled around the floor, she realized that neither one of them were bothering to count any longer. Emily had no idea if their dance would be considered graceful or elegant by anyone watching, but it was much more than one would ever believe of two people who had hardly ever danced the waltz before.

She didn't quite know how to describe it, but somehow, it just seemed... right.

10

"So tell me, Emily," Charles said, breaking the silence. "How does a woman such as you become a governess?"

"A woman such as me?" she repeated, blinking as she stared up at him.

He tightened the hand on her waist, drawing her closer to him before he even realized what he was doing. Now that there was but a foot between them, however, he wanted to see those sherry eyes again, allowing them to warm his soul, which had been frozen for so long.

But now those eyes were narrowed ever so slightly, as though he had said something to offend her. Why did his words never come out quite the way he meant them, particularly in her presence?

"I mean no offense," he said quickly. "It is just that you seem well-educated, well-spoken. I assume the 'Mrs.' in your name means that you were married once before, unless you added it to bring credence to your position."

"I assure you that it is not for any pretense," she said

with a slight smile. "I was married, yes," she paused, "he died six years ago."

"I'm sorry," he said, suddenly feeling like a reprobate for bringing it up when the outcome was rather obvious.

"It's fine," she said, her eyes taking on a faraway look, and she faltered a step for the first time since they had begun. "He and I had long been friends. When we reached our twenty-first birthdays, he offered for me. I hadn't met anyone else who struck my fancy, so I decided, why not? He was a barrister, like my father."

Charles thought he sensed some regret in her words, but he didn't comment upon it.

"Did you... enjoy your life together?"

"It was a good life, the few years it lasted," she said. "I spent my days enjoying Shakespeare and poetry, literature and history. His work allowed us to support my parents."

The music began to slow as the box began to wind down, and Emily stepped back out of his arms. Charles wished he had never started this conversation, for the moment of peace between them seemed to have been broken by this discussion of her past.

"Until he died," he murmured as he followed her across the room to where she took a seat on one of the blue brocade sofas that filled each room of the house. Apparently, Miriam had developed a fondness for them and became rather overzealous. Or perhaps she simply wanted an excuse to spend more of his money — he wasn't entirely sure.

"Until he died," she confirmed with a nod of her head. She wrung her hands together in her lap. "Oh, Charles, even now, I do feel rather guilty. For he was a good man, and we were happy together, as much as two people can be, I suppose. We were the greatest of friends, you could say.

After he passed, I knew I needed to work. My father was the grandson of a baronet, so he has some genteel upbringing, but he lost most of his money when the village bank lost everything. He is too old and ill to work, and my sister and I are the only children. She never married. So we both became governesses. We had enough family connections to provide us the background, and I managed to find an employer who pays better than most and treats me with kindness. The children are lovely."

Charles took a seat next to her on the sofa, leaning forward with his elbows on his knees so that he could clearly see her face.

"Are you happy?" he asked, looking at her intently and she blinked once more.

"With my employer?" She smiled wryly. "Why, Charles, are you looking to hire a governess?"

He sat back at her words. He hadn't meant that at all. He was asking if she was happy with her life, the life of a governess. Why he suddenly needed to know so desperately, he wasn't entirely sure.

"I am, but I do not think it would work, what with all believing that we are to be married."

"Ah, yes," she said, her cheeks flooding with pink as she looked down at her long, slender fingers, which were currently squeezing the fabric of the gown on her lap. "I had forgotten for a moment."

Charles stood, holding out a hand. "One more dance?"

"I really shouldn't," she said, standing as well, but backing up away from him. Suddenly, he felt the need to hold her closer; to be able to, perhaps, show her some comfort in this one way he could.

"Please?" he asked, and after staring at him for a moment, she nodded slowly.

"Very well."

He wound the box one more time, the familiar tune beginning again.

She placed her hand in his, and, their eyes locked, he drew her to him. Why did this woman, a governess, cause such turmoil within him? He had no time to be dancing with a woman in his saloon. He knew now that she was a competent, capable, if inexperienced, dancer. He settled his hands upon her once more, feeling the heat through the layers of clothing she wore. The new fabric of her dress was silky beneath his fingertips, and he congratulated himself on how well the garments fit her.

Unlike the many young ladies who seemed most desperately available to him, Emily had the generous curves of a woman. Her hip curved beneath his palm, and his fingers twitched with an unbidden urge to follow the swell of her buttocks to see how well it fit in his hand.

Stop it, Charles, he told himself. It had clearly been far too long since he had been with a woman, and now he was suffering the consequences, lusting after Emily Nicholls.

While he didn't enjoy the thought of a young woman nearly half his age in his bed, Emily was only but a year or so younger than he and had not given birth to a child during her married years. If his goal was to marry in order to produce an heir, then he'd best be looking elsewhere.

And it was not as though Emily had shown any interest in marrying *him*. For goodness sake, he had paid the woman in order to convince her to even keep up this charade for the next two weeks.

Heat flooded through him as he became rather embarrassed at the direction of his thoughts. This had all gone entirely wrong, simply because he had been too proud to allow his cousin a moment of triumph. And his family would be arriving tomorrow. Lord help him.

"Are you all right?" Emily's voice cut through his musings. "You seem rather... distracted."

"I am fine," he said quickly. Too quickly. "Just fine. Tell me, will you ever marry again?"

Emily's eyes widened at his words, and Charles could have kicked himself. Where had that question come from? It was certainly not one that should be directed at a woman, particularly within their current circumstances.

"I am not entirely sure," she said with a shrug of her shoulders. "Perhaps I will, if the opportunity arises. One can only work as a governess for so long. But it would have to be the right man, and I would have to... I don't know... *feel* something more this time. My first marriage was more of an arrangement, despite the fact that it was of our own choosing."

"I see," he said, concerned by the fact that he was relieved that she had not closed the door to marriage, that her first husband had not been the love of her life. Why did it matter? "You are an interesting woman, Emily."

She laughed, her head tilting back ever so slightly, and he found her merriment contagious, lightening his limbs. "That is kind of you, Charles, but I must say that *interesting* has never been a word used to describe me. In fact, most would say that I am rather boring. I enjoy reading. I do not provide interesting social conversation. I enjoy no hobbies that one would find any different than what others would aspire to. I often enjoy my own company more than anyone else's. I have no romantic stories and no interesting connections."

"Is that how you think of yourself?" he asked, tilting his head. "That is not what I see."

"No?" she asked, raising an eyebrow. "I was under the impression that when you selected me, I was simply a woman with whom you and your family were not acquainted and would serve your particular purpose."

"That is what I thought when I *first* saw you," he corrected.

"And now?"

"Now I see a woman who knows what provides her enjoyment in life. Who can bake the most amazing scones I have ever tasted while encouraging a young girl to open up to her. Who is intelligent enough to do what makes her happy while still looking after the responsibilities that were entrusted to her. Who can waltz with a gentleman she just met while hardly missing a step."

She didn't meet his gaze but he could tell by the way her cheeks slightly reddened and with the slight scrape of her teeth over her bottom lip that she was pleased with his words. He hadn't meant to embarrass her. He just thought she should know the truth, so that when she left here she would know that she was more than a typical governess.

"That is kind of you," she murmured, then smiled cheekily. "Be careful, Charles, or you might be mistaken for a romantic."

He laughed, which sounded rather rusty even to his own ears. He could not recall the last time he had found much to be overly humorous about. "A romantic I certainly am not. Nor, I believe, are you, Emily."

"No, I don't suppose I am," she said with a wistful sigh. "I do not believe that love can occur at first sight. I think flowers die far too soon for them to be considered a thoughtful gift. And I believe that many people marry before they truly understand who one another really is."

"As you did," he guessed.

"No," she countered. "I knew what type of marriage I was entering. I knew that we were friends, and would remain friends no matter what. We did not have a hot, passionate, fiery love that would only succeed in dying out one day."

"A fair point."

This was certainly not a typical conversation to be had with a lady, but with Emily, everything was different.

"Perhaps," she said with a shrug. "I have seen true love between my own parents, but it seems far more difficult to find than one might think. Forgive me, but it does not sound as if your own marriage was of such, Charles, so you can hardly argue with what I say."

"I suppose you are right," he said, thinking about Miriam. He thought he had fallen in love with her beauty, but he hadn't looked deeply enough beyond the surface. "But what if..."

The thought was not one that he should share with her. He had spoken without thinking beforehand which he never, ever did. This woman was causing his mind to become all muddled.

"What if what?" she asked, her voice just above a whisper, as though she wasn't entirely sure if she wanted him to finish the thought.

"What if you are wrong?" he finally uttered. "What if there *can* be both? Passionate love *and* friendship that will not disappear with time? Is such a thing possible?"

"I think one would have to be rather fortunate to find such a thing."

"Yes," he agreed, releasing her hand as the music slowed. But instead of stepping back, his hand came, unbidden, to the other side of her waist, and he ever-so-slowly pulled her closer toward him. "Yes, one would."

He tilted his head until their lips were but a breath away from one another. He shouldn't kiss her. It would only serve to further complicate their already unconventional relationship. One that had just begun and would have to serve them for another two weeks. They should stay friends — companions — just as she described.

But then her pink lips came slightly closer, and he couldn't help himself.

He bent and placed his lips upon hers, fusing them together. He waited for her to pull back, to push him away and tell him that this was folly, that the two of them didn't suit, that she was a governess and he an earl. It was exactly what he was thinking.

But she didn't do any of those things.

Instead, she kissed him back in equal measure, the kiss of a woman who knew what she wanted and knew exactly what she was doing. One of her hands rose to cup his cheek, and he nuzzled his head into that hand, taking from her all of the comfort she provided.

He palmed the back of her head, feeling her silken tresses beneath his fingertips, as though by holding her close he could become even more connected to her.

What was it about her that appealed to him? She was certainly qualified to be the perfect governess for his daughter, perhaps, but as a woman he might desire? He didn't know. Perhaps it was because she had managed to learn more about him in two days than any other woman ever had — even one who had been married to him for years. The only thing he knew for certain right now was that he was enjoying this more than he would ever care to admit.

He allowed his other hand to drift down to where it had been longing to go for some time now, and when he gripped her firm bottom, he felt more satisfaction than he had in quite some time. Oh, what would it feel like to be with her — to truly be with her?

The thought finally brought him back to his senses, and he lifted his mouth from hers, though he couldn't bring himself to completely leave her be. He rested his forehead against hers, his hands cupping the sides of her face.

"Tell me something, Charles," she said softly, and he nodded against her.

"Anything."

"I assume you are going to marry again?" she asked, and he tried not to jump in startlement. Was this where one kiss led?

"I will, yes," he said, slowly, ensuring he made no promises.

"Why?"

"Why?" he repeated. "Why would I marry again?"

"Yes."

"Well, I must produce an heir, in addition to providing someone to look after Margaret. That is the reason you and I became... acquainted, to keep my cousin from assuming that he or his son will become earl one day."

"Because you need an heir. Of course. That is what I thought," she said, stepping back from him. When she met his gaze, he was shocked by the sad smile that had replaced her usual warm expression. "Thank you, Charles, for the dances."

And with that, she turned and left the room. The only sound was the echo of her footsteps as he stood and stared after her, completely and utterly bewildered.

11

O h, but she was a fool.

Emily lay in the bed of her beautiful chamber, the likes of which she would never again sleep in after this Christmastide, and stared at the painted ceiling as she berated herself.

If she had thought she had an inkling of attraction for the man before, now... now she was completely and utterly besotted.

With an earl. A man who, if he ever remarried, would be to the daughter of an earl or a duke or a marquess or... anyone who was not a governess. And certainly not a woman of three-and-thirty, who had been married before and never became pregnant through the entire six-year union.

No, if there was ever a woman who would be entirely wrong for him, who he would never even consider for anything beyond a brief interlude, it was she.

It hurt far too much already, and she had to spend another thirteen days with the man.

What had she been thinking? Why would she ever think this was a good idea?

Because, some inner voice told her, *you didn't think that a romance like this could ever exist. You were under the impression that you would regard him simply as you would Lord Coningsby.*

But no, he was far more than that.

He might be far too serious, slow to show emotion, and not nearly as open to the love of his daughter as he should be. Yet... she could sense, deep down, that he craved more, that he simply didn't know how to be the man, and be the father, that he wanted to be. She had promised to help him in that regard. But now she wasn't sure how she could even be in the same room with him again.

That he had kissed her was obviously simply a moment in which he had forgotten himself. For she was most certainly not the type of woman he would ever be interested in for anything more than what would have been to him a meaningless kiss on the dance floor. He was an earl and not only that but an earl who was interested in finding himself a woman who would produce him an heir. That woman was certainly not her.

For one, she was near past the age in which a woman was most likely to bear children.

Then there was the fact that she had spent those very years married, and nothing had come of it. No children or even a hint of ever even conceiving. So no, she was not the woman he would likely ever choose to marry.

Besides that, he was free to wed any woman he wished. Emily had seen the vast number of beautiful young women of exceptional families who would likely be thrilled to become his countess.

So she must take these growing feelings for him and be done with them. She was not going to marry again, at least not to a man who would expect children. She had come to terms with the fact years ago that she wouldn't have children of her own. Now she had to learn that she could never be with a man who would want them as well. She must accept this and move on.

Perhaps it was time she left. But she quickly put aside that thinking as she remembered what she could now do for her own parents. And then there was Margaret.

Mayhap Charles would allow Margaret to come to visit her at the Coningsby's estate from time to time. Emily was sure she would get on well with the children there, and then she wouldn't be alone so frequently.

If nothing else, Emily vowed to take these next days here and do all she could to help Charles and Margaret repair their relationship. Then she would be gone, and all would return to what it had been before — what it should have remained.

At least, that was what she told herself as she finally drifted off to sleep.

THE NEXT MORNING dawned cold yet bright, and, clad in a high-necked hunter-green velvet gown that was fit for a lady of the highest order, Emily looked out her window at the snow that had begun to fall below.

It wasn't often that snow covered the ground on Christmas, but Emily thought it was rather beautiful on this Christmas Eve. She hoped it was a good omen for the day ahead. Charles' family would arrive tomorrow, but for today, Emily was intent on showing Margaret how much fun it could be to celebrate Christmas the way she knew how.

First, the decor.

Emily knew better than to ask Mrs. Graydon for any help, so after a breakfast in which she found herself alone, Emily sought out the butler.

"Toller!" she called when she caught him striding down a corridor. "I was hoping you could help me," she said once he came to a stop.

"Yes, my lady?" he asked, and Emily began to correct him upon his address of her, but then thought better of it after all that Charles had said to her regarding her status here in his home.

"I would like to decorate the house with some greenery," she said. "Could that be arranged?"

"Why the servants are already at work doing so," he said with some surprise. "Mrs. Graydon is directing them all in the marble hall."

"Oh, I see," she said, rather disappointed to find they were already well ahead of her. "Thank you, Toller. There is one other thing."

"Of course."

"I should like to select the Yule Log today."

"Oh, my lady," he said, concern etched on his face, his bushy eyebrows drawing together. "It is rather cold today, and much snow has fallen. Perhaps that is a job best left to the footmen and some of the tenants."

"I would be happy to be accompanied by a footman or two who could aid me," she said with what she hoped was a disarming smile. "They could return to fell the tree. However, I would like to take part in the selection. I enjoy it."

Toller bobbed his head, though Emily wasn't sure if she could call it a nod of agreement or more like an acknowledgment of her words. But eventually, he capitulated.

"Please advise when you are prepared, my lady," he said, and Emily beamed at him.

"Splendid," she said, grasping her hands together in front of her as she straightened her arms. "I look forward to it."

It was all she really had to look forward to, for she found when she entered the ballroom that Mrs. Graydon already had all well in hand, directing servants one way and the next, with no apparent role for Emily to play.

"Mrs. Nicholls!" Jenny called to her from across the ballroom, her arms full of festive decor and Emily smiled back at her temporary lady's maid, finding herself between two worlds, as she always had in her role as a governess.

The hall *was* looking rather fabulous already. Greenery wrapped around the marbled columns, with bows and berries fastened on the tree branches. When Emily entered the family quarters in her search for Margaret, she found the balconies were equally decorated.

Emily wasn't surprised that after a thorough search of the house, Margaret was ensconced in the music room, though it should have been the first place she thought of to look. Emily thought her suggestion of searching for a Yule Log would be met with excitement, but instead Margaret shook her head.

"Thank you, Mrs. Nicholls, but I would prefer to stay here," she said politely, and when Emily opened her mouth to insist, Margaret smiled at her and gently shook her head.

"I truly think it would be best," Margaret said. "It is rather cold outside, and I'm not one who likes the outdoors anyway. But please do not stay inside upon my account. I can tell you long to be out of doors, so please go. I don't much like the cold," she tilted her head, wrinkling her nose, "or snow."

Emily laughed. "Oh, very well, you've talked yourself out of it," she said. "But will you make me a promise?"

"What is that?"

"You will help light it when we return?"

"Of course!'" Margaret exclaimed with a smile, which Emily returned before beginning the journey back to her room for her cloak. With all of her walking around the manor, she would be nearly exhausted by the time she found this Yule Log, she figured with a laugh. When she was finally prepared, she sought out Toller once more, and he told her that he would have a footman meet her at the front entryway shortly.

Emily agreed and then left to complete one other task she had to accomplish before she found the log.

When she entered the marble hall, she was pleased to find that Mrs. Graydon was nowhere to be found. Emily perused the room, taking pieces of greenery, including evergreen, holly, mistletoe, rosemary, and bits of ribbon, placing them all on one of the tables that had been erected in the middle of the room, likely for organizing such things as she was about to do.

She began to weave together the various pieces, closing her eyes now and then to picture just how her mother did it year after year. She smiled as she reminisced of the many times she and her sister had attempted to be "accidentally" found beneath the mistletoe with the son of a neighbor who had stopped in. How silly they had been.

Her masterpiece complete, Emily was pleased to find Jenny, who had just returned from carrying a load of greenery. She promised Emily she would hang it exactly where Emily asked her to.

Now she just had to ensure that she was never caught anywhere near the thing, Emily thought with a bit of a laugh. It would be rather fun, however, to see who else may find themselves below it.

She pulled on her cloak, scarf, and earmuffs as she walked toward the front door, lifting the hood to cover her head and placing her hands in mittens to keep them warm from what she knew would be chilled air. She hoped the footman was one who would converse with her and not keep to the silence that was so expected of men of his station. Alas, she figured Charles had that effect upon most of his staff, but that was hardly her fault, now was it?

When she reached the doors, however, she stopped short. For there *was* a tall, dark-haired, strong handsome man awaiting her. But it wasn't a footman.

"Charles," she said, looking up at him as she gripped her mittened hands together. "What are you doing?"

"Waiting for you," he said growling. "You took some time to arrive."

"I was not aware that we had an arrangement," she said, swallowing hard. She had actually been pleased that they hadn't crossed paths yet that day, so confused she was by her reaction to him after their dance and kiss last night. "I apologize, but I have something else I need to do."

"Search for a Yule Log?" he asked, raising one eyebrow, and it was only then that she noticed he was dressed similarly to her, with a long black cloak covering all of his clothing underneath, a warm fur hat upon his head.

"Yes," she said slowly.

"So I heard. But I can hardly allow you to traipse about the property in the growing snow by yourself."

"I was going with a footm—"

"With a footman. Yes, I am aware. I hardly think it is appropriate for you to be wandering the property alone with a footman. Therefore, as you seem stubborn enough to continue to pursue this idea, I will go with you."

"Oh, Charles, you really mustn't. I know you are not exactly enthralled with the idea of searching for a Yule Log."

"Nor am I *enthralled* with the idea of you going alone."

She said nothing, for he was right. She was determined to go, whether or not she was alone. She might not be with her family this Christmas, but if she had to remain far from them, at the very least she could keep their traditions alive.

Charles held out his arm to her.

"Shall we?"

12

C harles looked down at the woman walking beside him. Her cheeks and the tip of her nose were pink with cold, while her spectacles kept slightly frosting over from the steam of her breath before returning to their clear state. The heavy snow fell around her face, dusting her cap and the shoulders of her cape with a layer of white flakes, just as they did the evergreens that were beginning to crowd around them the farther they walked into the wood beyond Ravenport.

"Are you cold, Emily?" he asked as their boots created indents in the deepening snow.

"No," she said, though her lie was obvious as her teeth were beginning to slightly chatter. He carried a piece of cloth that they intended to tie around the selected tree for the groundskeeper to return and fetch along with a couple of footmen.

"I'm not entirely sure what was wrong with any of the dozens of trees we have passed so far," he said dryly.

"They were not the right width," she said crisply. "And

besides that, I didn't want to mar any of the trees that were visible from the manor itself."

"That is considerate of you, but I assure you, unnecessary. I hardly think anyone will notice anything missing from one of the many trees upon this property."

The look she sent him out of the corner of his eye worried him, for he sensed it meant that she either didn't appreciate his words or was planning for much more than a branch. She didn't, however, comment. Instead, she simply went back to searching out the trees around her.

Charles wasn't entirely sure how to best approach Emily after what had happened between them last night. He hadn't been able to sleep after their kiss and when he did, it was only to dream of her.

She was witty, she was frank, she was intelligent, and she was more alluring than he wanted to admit.

He hadn't noticed it at first. Had barely noticed *her*, if he was honest. When she had caught his eye, it was simply because she was the first woman he saw. But after spending the last couple of days together, she had revealed so much more within her that he found his desire to know her better ever growing — and for more reasons than simply to convince his family that the two of them would soon be wed.

Yet she apparently did not seem inclined to further what they had started last night. She held herself away from him. Her fingers had just lightly rested upon his arm as they had walked from Ravenport, and once they reached the path leading into the wood she had dropped her hand completely, instead focused on scouring the trees in her quest.

"When was the last time you searched for a Yule Log?"

she asked, though her voice did not contain much interest and he assumed she was simply making conversation.

"Never."

"Never?" she whirled toward him in shock. "Not even when you were a youth?"

He chuckled. "No, Emily. That is a job for the groundskeeper or for some of the tenants. Not for the earl and his children."

"I am sorry," she said, continuing to walk forward, her hands clasping behind her back. "I know I have rather bungled this role I am playing, but I cannot say that deception comes easily."

"And you think it does for me?" he asked, slightly insulting by her insinuation. "This situation was born of necessity."

"Or pride."

"Pardon me?" he asked, unsure if he had heard her correctly and rather hoping he hadn't.

"My apologies, Charles. It simply seems to me that this entire charade grew out of your desire for your cousin not to feel that he had any hold over you or Ravenport."

Charles was silent, as he had no response to that. For she was right.

"This will do," she finally said, staring up at the tree in front of her. The oak looked as though it hadn't had a particularly fruitful summer season. If they didn't cut it down, it was likely to die soon enough anyway.

"Are you sure?" he asked, wondering if it was a good omen to use a dying tree for a Yule Log.

"I am," she said with a curt nod. "It has served its purpose, and now it can move on to another."

"The entire tree?" he questioned, assessing its width.

"The entire tree," she confirmed.

"Very well," he said, lifting the scarf in his hands and tying it around the tree. "Now to return and let Toller know where to send the men and the horses, if necessary."

They turned around, and Charles was shocked to see just how far in the distance Ravenport loomed. In fact, it was barely visible through the falling, swirling snow. They had traveled much farther than he had anticipated.

"Oh dear," she said, apparently coming to the same conclusion as her head appeared beside him, as high as his shoulder. He was a tall man, and she a mite shorter than what would be average height for a woman, though she made up for her height with her curves, as he had discovered last night.

"Can you make it?" he asked, and she nodded, though she did not look overly confident. The snow was falling faster now and a slight wind had picked up, swirling it in front of them. The footsteps that he had assumed would lead them back to the manor were erased, as though they had never walked this way to begin with.

They were trudging through heavy snow and even Charles was freezing, his feet like icicles as the snow soaked through his boots and stockings underneath.

He looked at Emily once more, and her cheeks had now reddened, her teeth chattering so fiercely it was as though they were drumming the beat for one of Margaret's melodies.

"You look as though you are nearing frostbite."

"I'm fine."

"You are not fine."

"Well, I do not have much choice in the matter, do I?" she asked fiercely, her tone cross, though he figured it was likely more so due to anger at her own decisions rather than directed at him.

"We actually do have a choice," he said after a moment of considering their options. "There is a cabin close to here, used by the gamekeeper in the warmer weather."

"So close to the manor?"

"My father enjoyed a good hunt. I find I have far more things to occupy myself with and, besides our annual family Christmas gathering, I haven't hosted a house party in some time."

"Well..." she said with one final look toward Ravenport. Charles noted that her lips were turning a shade closer to purple than their usual pink. "Perhaps we could stop for a moment to warm up before returning."

"Very well," he said. The timing could not be more perfect as he saw the opening in the trees to where the cabin was located. Besides that, he didn't want to admit just how cold he had become himself. This winter storm had rolled in fast. He wondered whether any of his company would be able to reach his home, which could be the one saving grace of such weather.

"It's through here," he said, and when she stumbled ever so slightly, he knew he had to get her there as quickly as possible. He crouched down and placed an arm underneath her knees, lifting her up.

"Oh!" she exclaimed as he did so, her arms coming to his chest in order to balance herself. "Charles, what are you doing?"

"You can barely walk," he said, noting that he needed to partake in more physical activity than he had as of late. "I'm helping you."

"Put me down," she said, her voice full of authority, but he was not one of the children she commanded.

"Don't be foolish, woman," he said in answer, showing her that an earl could have just as much power as a governess. She gasped but was helpless to fight him. He sensed her surrender when her body lost some of its rigidness and one of her arms came around his neck.

It was, thankfully, a short walk through the wood, and he breathed a sigh of relief when the cabin came into sight. He finally set her down when they approached the door, though he smiled smugly to himself at the fact that she kept one hand braced on his arm.

The door was unlocked though it fit rather tightly in the jam, and he had to shoulder it open. The hinges squeaked as the door finally began to move, and he practically tumbled in with Emily close behind him.

It was a small, one-room cottage, with a fireplace on one side of the room, a single bed on the other, and near the door was the smallest of desks with a wooden chair in front of it, where the gamekeeper would sometimes update a ledger of what animals were to be found in the hunting grounds.

Charles walked over to the desk and found a tinderbox to light the grate to help them warm up. He was grateful logs had been laid on the fireplace, likely from the last time the gamekeeper had been there.

"Why don't you take the blanket from the bed?" he murmured, but when he turned, he found that Emily was already sitting upon it with her boots and stockings on the floor, her legs tucked up beneath her, and the blanket wrapped around her. She held her spectacles between her fingers by their arms, spinning them around. They must have become quite foggy from the change in air temperature.

"I see you've made yourself at home," he noted as the flames began to lick the logs.

"Actually, this is the most at home I've felt on your entire estate," she said with a slight chuckle, though he could hear the wistfulness in her voice.

Charles crossed the room and sat next to her on the worn yet clean bed, ensuring he maintained a respectful distance between them. He looked down at his hands clasped in his lap.

"I must apologize for taking you from your family this Christmas," he said slowly, wanting to make sure she understood that he was serious. "I do appreciate what you are doing for me."

She looked away, and he sensed that she was somewhat embarrassed by his words.

"You made an offer that I couldn't refuse, don't forget."

He smiled then, chuckling slightly as he looked up at the low ceiling, made of rough-hewn timber like the rest of the cottage. He had no idea how long the small building had stood, but it was likely longer than the manor house itself. Actually, he wondered if, at one time, this had been a more remote part of the estate, as the original manor was much farther away, at the outskirts of what was now his land.

"I must seem ridiculous to you — paying you to act as my future wife, and for no reason really, than to keep myself from being proven wrong," he said, standing now and striding across the room to hold his hands out in front of the fire, attempting to cover how self-conscious he felt in front of her.

"Not at all," she said, her voice coming closer as she must have stood and was now walking toward him. "We all make decisions in the moment that we sometimes later regret. Would you — would you like me to leave? Your estate, I mean, this house party. Not this cottage at the moment, for I fear I really do need to warm some before we return."

He turned to her now, finding that she had come closer than he'd realized. Her face was tilted up toward him as she waited for his answer, the fire's flames casting light to dance off the planes of her face. He noted the tiniest of freckles dotted her pert nose. He had an unrestricted view into her eyes now, and he reached out to stroke the top of her cheekbones with his thumbs as his other fingers wrapped around her jaw.

"No," he shook his head slowly as his finger stroked the soft skin of her face. "It may make me a selfish man, Emily, but I very much do not want you to be anywhere but here."

13

Emily shivered, but this time it was not with cold.

She was trembling all right, but it was from the touch of Charles' fingers upon her face, of his nearness, of the fact that she was standing with him in front of a fire, alone in a cottage when no one knew where they were.

It was quite scandalous. It was exactly the situation she had told herself to avoid. And yet, despite her offer to leave, she didn't want to be anywhere but here.

"Charles," she said, swallowing, needing to put space between them. She could hardly see his face in front of her, so atrocious was her vision without her spectacles, but she could see enough to know how seriously he was looking at her, how intent his eyes were focused on her face, how firmly he gripped her arms. It seemed everything this man did was with determined precision. She searched her mind wildly for something to say. "Are your feet not cold?"

"Pardon me?" he said, his eyebrows lifting as her words were apparently not what he was expecting to hear.

She took a breath, and his musky scent of ink and

leather drifted into her nostrils, overcoming the mustiness of the cottage which had obviously not been used in some time.

"I— I asked if your feet are not cold as well," she said, feeling the fool but forging ahead anyway. "My feet were soaked from the snow. Are yours not?"

"Slightly," he said, his hands drawing down from her face now and she missed his touch, wishing she had said nothing that would cause him to rethink where they had been. "But they don't seem to be overly bothering me at the moment."

"Mine are like icicles," she said, telling the truth.

"Come," he said, taking her hand and leading her the two steps over to the bed, careful not to sit on her spectacles. He lifted them carefully and placed them on the floor beside them. "Give me your feet." He held out his hands to her.

"Oh, I couldn't," she said, the back of her neck and her face beginning to tingle as her breathing quickened.

"I will not tell anyone," he promised, but she shook her head.

"It isn't that," she said, biting her lip.

"Then why not?"

"Because... it simply doesn't seem... right."

"Hush," he said, obviously not wanting to discuss it any further. He kept his hands outstretched toward her, offering her no choice but to reach her leg out to him. Her toes looked small and pale in comparison to his large hands, and as cold as she was, heat rose in her cheeks as he palmed her feet.

But then he began to rub them to infuse warmth back in, and she forgot all of her shyness as blood began rushing into her extremities once more.

"Oh!" she exclaimed. "That... hurts!"

"Just focus on the feeling of my fingers," he murmured, and now he moved from rubbing her toes to massaging the rest of her foot. His thumbs kneaded into the pad at the bottom, moving down over the arch, to her heel and back. When he had finished treating one foot, he switched over to the next. The initial rush to her toes was now replaced by the loveliest sensations Emily could imagine. She couldn't recall anyone ever paying such sweet attention to her in this way. For a man who came off as rather cold and standoffish, he was showing more care than she could ever have imagined.

She opened her eyes now to find that his hard face was concentrating on her feet to the same extent as he would were he reviewing a ledger in front of him. The fact that he, the Earl of Doverton, would care enough to not only stop here for her when he had a house party awaiting him but to devote such care for her... it melted her heart as well as her toes.

"Thank you," she said, her voice just over a whisper, and he shook his head slightly.

"It was my own fault. I should have made sure we turned back sooner."

"You cannot take responsibility for everything on yourself. I was being stubborn," she admitted. "I was trying so hard to make sure what was in my control was perfect, and in doing so I caused us to enter into this predicament."

"I'm sure there's enough blame to be had that we can share it," he said, then set her feet to the side to stand and pick up her boots and stockings. He carried them over to the front of the fire, laying them out in front of it. Then he unlaced his own boots and set them beside hers.

She stood, wrapped the blanket around her, and waited for him to turn and look at her.

"Thank you," she said softly.

"For what?"

"For accompanying me into the woods. For being patient with me while I was being irrational in selecting just the perfect tree. For knowing I was cold. For carrying me to this cottage. For staying here with me when I know there is so much else that requires your attention. For... caring."

He leaned down closer to her, drawing the blanket farther over her shoulders and wrapping it even more snugly around her.

"You make it too easy to care," he whispered, "for one only needs to follow your lead."

Emily was ready this time and urgently waiting for his kiss. His lips touched hers for a moment, ever so softly. He leaned back and looked at her as though questioning whether or not this was the right decision. She nodded, and then when he returned his lips to hers, it was with the fiery passion she had come to know from him before.

As hard as his lips pressed upon hers, his hands were feather soft as they teased her, running down her arms, up her back, and lightly caressing her neck. She melted into them, the blanket falling down at her feet as she dropped it to bring her arms up around his neck. He was just so very... male.

As a woman who had been married before, Emily, of course, understood the interaction between man and woman, the intimacies of coming together in the most physical of acts.

But what she hadn't understood was the desire that could exist between two people. With James, it had been a matter of duty, of obligation. She had enjoyed it *enough*, but it wasn't... like this.

Charles might appear cold and standoffish, but this man currently holding her? He was anything but cold.

His fingers, which seemed to be everywhere at once, drifted up her stomach, and she sucked in a breath at the sensations as they journeyed over her bodice to the ties of her cloak. He slowly undid the bow she had fashioned, until the tendrils of the ribbon that drifted down upon her bosom seemed like they were tickling her with their touch.

The cloak followed the blanket to the floor, and she deftly undid his with one quick tug. A slight growl emerged from his throat and he cupped the back of her head, tilting it to one side, which allowed him better access to her mouth. His tongue teased her lips until he all but demanded entrance, and soon the dance between them was one of tasting, exploring, giving and taking all at once.

"Emily," he murmured, and she responded by pressing the length of her body against him, reveling in all of his rigid contours, which contrasted so dramatically with her own softness yet fit perfectly against it at the same time.

"What are you doing to me?" he asked when he leaned his head back away from her for a moment. "This isn't supposed to happen."

"No," she said fiercely, wholeheartedly agreeing with him. "But happening it is."

"This is a terrible idea."

"You are right."

But her nod was all the encouragement he needed to resume where they had left off.

Only this time, instead of focusing on their kiss alone, his hands wandered farther south, until they were playing with the delicate lace that bordered the bodice of the dress that he had bought for her. His thumbs drifted lower, grazing her nipples, and Emily arched into his touch, practically begging for more. She felt wanton, but it was... delicious.

"I need to see you," he murmured into her mouth. "To *feel* you."

"Then see me you shall," she said softly, shyly, taking his hand within hers and pulling him back the foot to the bed. When she had been married, it had been very seldom that her husband had seen her undressed. The times they had been together had typically been beneath the covers, a quick, efficient joining in the dark.

Not like this.

Emily turned around for Charles to access the buttons on the back of her dress. She was used to gowns which allowed her to undress herself. She still wasn't quite used to requiring a maid to undress her.

Charles made fairly quick work of the buttons, though he did not seem to be a master seducer. Emily's heart began to beat faster as fear began to take root and grow. What would Charles think when he saw her undressed? Would this be as far as the two of them would go, she wondered as she slowly began to turn toward him, clad now only in her chemise. James had never been particularly enthused to see her without any clothing. Would Charles think her too wide? Too voluptuous? Too pale? Too—

"You're perfect," he said, his voice somewhat breathless as his eyes darkened with desire. All of Emily's fears and doubts began seeping away. The space they left behind was filled with her own desire for Charles. There was still so much unresolved between them, and no promise for anything further to come, but for now, Emily would have to be satisfied with having this brief moment in time with him.

Just for today, she could imagine that they were beginning a life with one another. That their betrothal was not contrived but rather as true as she could ever imagine.

For today, this Christmas Eve, he was hers.

He hadn't been formally dressed underneath his cloak, and she longed to feel his bare skin upon hers. She pushed his jacket off of his shoulders, undoing his buttons until she could lift his shirttails free from his breeches, allowing him to pull it over his head.

And then her fingers were free to explore him as he had her. She inched her fingertips along his chest, exploring the contours of his muscles beneath his skin, so much darker in contrast to hers. She brushed a light touch over the coarse hair that dusted his chest, appreciating all of the differences between them.

Then she no longer had any time to think as he lifted her up against him, cradling her in his arms as he had when he carried her across the room. He set her down gently on the bed, but then his time for tenderness seemed to vanish, replaced by passion that had ignited in him, as stormy as the snow falling outside of the cabin.

Emily waited for his kiss, but instead of it landing on her lips, he began to kiss down the side of her neck, over her collarbones to her nipples, which were longing for his touch. He caressed one with his mouth, the other with his fingers until she was nearly straining off the bed as her body began to crave more.

Then he lifted himself from her long enough to untie her stays and then gather the clothing that remained bunched at her waist and slide it down off of her legs. He paused for a moment and Emily opened one eye, peeking up at him. But soon he had inched down her body, following the garments, until he was teasing the nub of her very center. She gasped in surprise — James would *never* have even considered such a thing — but then all thought was chased from her mind as the sensations of her climax began to course through her.

Charles apparently felt it too, for he slid into her, filling her and completing her in one breath. She lifted her hips to invite him in further, and his moan told her that he was as equally fulfilled as she at how they fit together.

They soon found their rhythm, and it wasn't long before he began to groan her name, slightly biting her shoulder as he slowed and purposefully drove into her.

"Emily!" he cried out once more as he withdrew from her body and spilled his seed onto the sheets of the bed beside her.

Even as she lay there as sated as could possibly be, a lone tear fell from Emily's eye. For his actions were unnecessary. And the reason was the same as to why they could never truly remain together.

14

Never before had he felt so complete.

Charles lay on his side, his head propped up on his elbow as he stared down at Emily Nicholls, who lay on her back beside him on the bed that was made for only one, but was, at the moment, just the perfect size.

Her sandy-blond hair was fanned out behind her on the sheet. He couldn't quite recall if he had removed the pins from her hair, or if it had fallen out of its own accord, but he now appreciated the view of the length of it hanging around her. It curled slightly, he noticed, picking up a few strands and wrapping them around his finger.

Her cheeks were pink, her lips a bruised red from their lovemaking, and now he traced the slightest of indents on her shoulder, which his teeth had found at the very end.

She had been most enthusiastic, and yet... it was only then that he saw the tear leaking from her eye, making its way over her temple to spill on the thin pillow below it.

"I'm so sorry," he said urgently, guilt assaulting him. "That never should have happened. I took advantage—"

"No, no," she said, shaking her head emphatically,

holding up a finger. "Do not say that. Do not think that. That was perfect. And I was as willing a participant as anyone could ever be."

"I'm glad to hear it," he said, though he was still quite worried. "But what saddens you, then?"

She sniffed slightly.

"It's nothing to worry about," she said, a clearly forced smile covering her face now. "That was wonderful, Charles, truly."

"Will you not share with me?" he asked, not entertaining her words. "Please, Emily."

She was silent for a moment, and he rose from the bed just long enough to find the blanket she had shed not long ago, and he covered her with it to keep her from becoming chilled once more.

"I'm a thirty-three-year-old widow," she said, not meeting his eye. "I work to provide for my aging parents. I spend my days taking care of children but have none of my own, despite how much I would dearly love to. And I never will."

The guilt within Charles only dug itself deeper, though the reasoning behind it shifted.

"Thirty-three is not too old to have children," he managed in an effort to comfort her, but she shook her head, her long locks moving with her across the pillow.

"It is if one was married for six years and never once became pregnant," she said with a sigh. "No, for whatever reason, Charles, God did not see fit to provide me with a child. And that would be fine, I think, if I had known love in another form. If I had married a man who loved me for who I was and not just because he needed a bride and we knew one another well."

Charles felt a pang deep within his chest as he remembered all that he had said to her — his need for a wife to bear him an heir, the fact that he wouldn't marry for any other reason. How he must have insulted her.

"I'm sorry, Emily, for—"

"You have nothing to be sorry for," she said adamantly. "I was the one who agreed to come here, knowing what I did. I was the one who foolishly stayed here, allowing myself to become close to another child, to another man. I was the one who caused us to be alone here together, who craved making love to you, despite knowing how this will end."

"And how do you think it will end?" he asked, needing to know exactly how she felt, despite what his mind told him — that he shouldn't even ask, for it couldn't lead to anything but pain for the two of them.

She sat up now, pulling the blanket around her tightly so that he couldn't see any more of her, despite how much he yearned to.

"It will end with the two of us clothing ourselves, leaving here when we can make it through the snow, and returning to your massive, extravagant estate where I don't belong except in the capacity of servant or governess. Your family will arrive. For the next week, I will put a smile on my face and pretend that I am your doting bride. I will help you spend time with Margaret, and the two of you will become close. Then I will return to Lord and Lady Coningsby's estate, and you will tell your family it did not work out between us but you have found a much more suitable bride — for you will. That is how it will end."

She said the words so matter-of-factly, so monotone, that he found himself longing for her typical cheerful enthusiasm. If he had known that making love to her would result in this, then he never would have done it — would he?

For being with her had been the most gratifying, exhilarating experience of his entire life. While she may look exactly the part she played of governess, she exuded a passion that was held deep within her.

When he had first kissed her, he thought this would be fleeting. When she had told him that she had wanted to make love to him, he had thought that perhaps if they had this time together, he would find his desire for her sated, would be able to move on and discover what else was awaiting him.

But now that he had been with her, he only wanted more. She was to him like whiskey was to a drunkard.

"I... I don't want it to end like that," he said, surprising both of them with his words.

"Then how do you see it ending?" she asked with a shaky voice.

"I don't know," he said, raising his hands to the side. "But that cannot be all."

"I certainly will not be your mistress," she said somewhat indignantly. "And you have made it clear that I cannot be your wife."

"Perhaps you could become pregnant..." he said, hardly believing what he was saying. Would he... *could* he actually marry her?

"But most likely I will not," she said fiercely. "Could you live with that?"

He listened to the wind howling outside the window, thought of the lands that surrounded them, the estate that she slightly mocked but he secretly loved, lying just up the hill beyond them. It would all become his cousin's, and then his cousin's son's property.

He could hardly stomach the thought. He had always imagined he would be passing down all he had to a son who would carry on the legacy he had created, who would look after his tenants and keep the peaceful, prosperous estate just how he had left it behind. He had worked so hard to make it what it was today.

Was it worth giving up all of that for a woman he had come to know for a few short days? A woman who, for all intents and purposes, was no one he should be attracted to, and was altogether wrong for him?

He looked over at her now, meeting her eyes, which had taken on an inscrutable look.

"You don't have to answer that," she said in response to his silence, her voice heavy and husky.

"It's just—"

"It's fine."

"It's not."

It was just that he had no idea how to answer her.

"Your company will likely be arriving soon," she said despondently. "Will they not be wondering where we are? Oh dear, and Margaret. What could she be thinking?"

"We will return soon. Hopefully someone will come looking for us," he assured her. "We aren't far. Though we'd best get dressed."

They dressed in near silence, as the images of the clothes coming off flickered through Charles' mind.

"I do appreciate all you have done for me," he managed, and she nodded, a tight smile on her face.

"I know, Charles."

He watched as she crouched and began to search the floor.

"Is there anything I can help with?" he asked as he listened to her mutter, which he had to admit was rather endearing.

"My glasses," she said. "I cannot find them anywhere."

"Can you see much without them?" he asked.

"Nearly nothing at all," she said with a sigh. "It is rather tiresome."

"I can imagine," he said as he quickly found them in the corner. He lifted them and brushed the dust away, for they had collected much of it from sitting in the corner.

"Here," he said, gently placing them back upon her nose, allowing her eyes to focus on him once he did so. "All put back together."

"Thank you," she said softly, and for a moment when their eyes met, all seemed that it was as it should be, the two of them together. She seemed to understand him. To fit with him. To fill in the pieces that were missing.

Perhaps—

There was a loud knocking on the door.

"My lord? Are you in there?"

"Just in time," Charles murmured as he bestowed one last smile upon Emily and crossed to the door, a gust of wind hitting him in the face as he opened it. The groundskeeper and two of Charles' tenants were standing outside in the blowing snow, and Charles quickly waved them in.

"We were waiting for your return," the groundskeeper said, "and became worried when you didn't come back. It was hard to follow your tracks, but I saw the scarf on the tree and then thought to check here. We've brought the sled so that Mrs. Nicholls could ride in it on the way back."

"Oh, I'm fine," Emily said from the chair, where she was lacing up her boots, but Charles held up a hand.

"You will ride in the sleigh," he said firmly before turning back to the men. "And what of the tree?"

"Oh, Charles," Emily said from behind him. "I hardly think—"

"It's Christmas Eve," he interrupted her. "If the lady wants a Yule Log, then a Yule Log she shall have."

"Very well," the groundskeeper said. "Shouldn't take long with the three of us."

"The four of us," Charles countered, "for I will help you."

"No, no, my lord," the groundskeeper protested, but Charles was firm. He was the lord here, and if he chose to help fell the Yule Log, then that's what was going to happen.

He also had some unfounded perverse sense of needing to do this himself, with his own hands, as a gift for Emily. Which was a strange notion, as he paid these men very well to do such a service for him, but he couldn't shake the feeling.

And so it was, in the biting wind and the painful cold, the two horses, four men, and Emily returned to the manor an hour later with the Yule Log in tow. Charles was tired and cold, but then he saw the look on Emily's face as they approached the manor. She was smiling, and when he followed her gaze, he saw that the object of her affection was standing in the doorway waiting for them. Margaret. She was hopping up and down with excitement, her dark chocolate glossy hair bouncing upon her shoulders as she watched them come. The sun was just beginning to set, and she looked like an angel with a halo of light from the wall sconce behind her head.

The cold and his exhaustion no longer mattered. What did was the beautiful little girl — *his* little girl — and the woman in the sleigh beside him.

This was what family felt like, he realized.

And for the first time in his life, Charles had a glimpse of what Christmas was truly all about.

15

"My Lord, Lord and Lady Bishop and Lord and Lady Fredericton have arrived," Toller announced, stepping back to allow the two couples to enter. It was quite late that night, and Charles hadn't even been sure if his cousins would brave the cold to arrive. It had all worked out for the best, however, for they had been so late getting back from their... excursion. Emily's cheeks reddened just thinking about it.

Now was not the time to allow her mind to wander there, however, for she had Charles' family to deal with. The lords were a few years older than their wives, who looked like sisters. Emily stepped back even farther toward the wall as the couples entered. She wished she could disappear entirely, blending in with the wallpaper behind her. But, alas, her navy dress was not quite the color of the sky-blue wallpaper. Perhaps they wouldn't notice her. If she stood just to the side, then maybe the giant cream vase would hide her well enough so that no one would—

"Charles, Edward told us you are getting *married* again! Oh, this must be her!"

Apparently, Edward had told them who to look for.

Charles followed his cousins over toward Emily as she attempted a smile that would appease them.

"Lady Bishop and Lady Fredericton," Charles said, his own smile looking rather strained. "May I present Mrs. Nicholls?"

"Oh, no need to be so formal, Charles," Lady Bishop said, as the two of them looked down at Emily as though she were a specimen to be beheld. Both women had the same dark hair as Charles and their brother Edward. They were slim with beautiful gowns draped over them. Emily rather envied their conventional beauty, and wished she knew exactly what to say to them. She had been versed in polite conversation, but she had a feeling this would go much beyond that.

"We are Anita and Katrina, my dear."

"A pleasure to meet you," Emily said, wishing she were far from here — in fact, wishing that she was about nine miles down the road, sitting at her parents' kitchen table, instead of being spoken to as though she were a child. She must be nearly the same age as these women.

"Edward has told us all about you, Mrs. Nicholls," Lady Fredricton said — at least, Emily thought it was Lady Fredericton. The sisters were so similar in looks, though one had what Emily assumed was a painted mole beside her lip. "We nearly didn't come today, what with the weather as it is, but I am *so* glad we decided to take the sleigh and were able to arrive in time for Christmas. We can hardly wait to learn more about you. Tell us, where are you from?"

"From Newport."

"So close. I wonder if we have any mutual acquaintances," Lady Bishop said, a finger coming to her lips as she tilted her head to contemplate Emily. "While we are in

London a fair bit, our home is near Cambridge so we know many of the noble families in the area. I'm sure there must be some of our friends who you would have met."

"I doubt it," Emily said as pleasantly as she could, but they continued on as though they hadn't heard her.

"Lady Smythe?"

"Lady Anderson?"

"Lady Endicott?" they questioned one after the other as Emily continued to shake her head.

"At one point in time, a barrister from Newport represented the family — Mr. Nowell, his name was — but I do hope you are not associated with them, as I've heard they lost everything," Lady Fredericton said, lowering her voice to whisper conspiratorially.

Emily blanched at her words, for the man she spoke of was her father. She didn't exactly wish to discuss such a thing with them or allow it to be known, but neither would she allow her family's name to remain on the lips of the gossips.

"Actually," she began, but just then Toller interrupted them once more.

"Mr. and Mrs. Blythe," he announced to the room, and Emily heard Charles mutter something indistinguishable under his breath when he heard his cousin Edward had arrived. "Oh, and Mr. Thaddeus Blythe," Toller added as he backed out of the doorway.

So this was the family who would take over Ravenport one day unless Charles produced an heir, Emily mused as she looked them over. She had seen more than she would have wished of Edward Blythe at the Coningby's ball, of course, but she hadn't seen the son.

"Edward, Letitia, how wonderful to see you!" Lady

Bishop said, crossing the room to greet her brother and his wife, Lady Fredericton quickly following suit.

"I'm sorry, Emily, truly I am," Charles said quietly after they had walked away, but Emily waved a hand in the air, signaling to him that it was of no consequence.

"This is why I'm here," she said, her words sounding far more confident than she felt.

"Mrs. Nicholls!" Edward said, coming directly toward them. He walked with an air of confidence. He looked much like Charles, though his hair had far more silver streaks, and where Charles stood tall and proper, his face typically a mask of stoicism, Edward's was wreathed in what Emily felt was an insincere smile that was currently quite smug. "How *wonderful* to see you again," he said. "Leticia and I were wondering if you would be here this Christmas."

"And just why would she not be?" Charles asked, his eyes hard as he looked at his cousin.

"No reason, Charles, none at all," he said, the smirk remaining on his face.

"My, that is a lovely gown, Mrs. Nicholls," Mrs. Blythe said. She was tall and blond, her eyes an icy blue, her figure as slim as Emily's was rather round. "From what Edward told me—"

"Thank you, Mrs. Blythe," Emily cut in, not wanting to create a disturbance but in equal measure having no wish to be looked down upon by the woman nor discuss her former wardrobe. "Charles has been very generous."

"Oh, and you must meet our son," Mrs. Blythe continued as though Emily had never spoken. "Thaddeus!"

The young man wandered over, his eyes bored, his steps unhurried as he clearly had no wish to be at a Christmas party with only family in attendance. "Thaddeus, this is Mrs. Nicholls. She is to marry Lord Doverton."

"Pleasure," he said lazily, and Emily could practically feel Charles' disapproval. The young man was certainly handsome, and Emily could see why he perhaps had a reputation as a rogue. "I'm going for a quick stroll," he said, looking at his parents. "All right?"

"Very well, Thaddeus," his mother said, her lips pursed in displeasure, but she obviously didn't want to create a scene with all of them looking on. "Oh, Thaddeus!" she called after him and then leaned in to whisper in his ear, though Emily's hearing, honed from years of looking after her charges, caught something regarding the maids.

She caught Charles' eye and raised an eyebrow slightly, though she did wish that he would erase his frown. He looked as though he'd rather be anywhere but in this room — which was likely true, but Emily did yearn for some inkling of the man she had been with just that afternoon.

"Charles," she said, sensing both of them needed a distraction. "Perhaps now is the time to light the Yule Log? I'm sure Margaret would like to join us."

"Ah, yes," he said with some relief. "I'll have a footman fetch Toller."

"I'll find him," she said, having no wish to be left alone with his family members. She quickly walked away before he could stop her, searching out the butler who was blessedly just outside of the drawing room.

She explained to him that they were going to light the Yule Log, and could he please bring in the tinder for Lord Doverton? She was going to ask him to find Lady Margaret to join them, but then decided she would do so herself, for it wouldn't be difficult to find the girl.

She was right — Margaret was alone in the music room, but a smile came to her face when Emily asked her to join them.

It saddened Emily to think that it was Christmas Eve and the little girl had been expecting to spend it all alone.

"Oh, Margaret, it will be such fun," she said enthusiastically. "Your father is going to light the Yule Log."

"The Yule Log?" she repeated, her face solemn. "I have never been part of the lighting before. The servants have always done it."

"Well, you are in for a treat," Emily said. "And your family is looking forward to seeing you."

"Oh," Margaret said, her face falling. "I don't like them very much."

"No?" Emily asked, keeping her voice steady and her face impassive. "Why ever not?"

"They ignore me, just like my father," she said with a sigh. "They speak in loud voices throughout the house all night long. And the youngest one, he scares the maids."

"I see," Emily said, nodding, her heart breaking for the girl. She could see why Charles was concerned about Thaddeus. Emily knew far more than she could ever wish to about young noblemen who took advantage of the servants.

"Well, I am excited to be the one to tell you that your father has reserved the place of honor for you," she said. "*You* will stand beside him while he lights it."

Emily saw a flicker of interest in Margaret's eye, but she quickly looked away as she joined Emily for the long trek back to the drawing room.

The girl slipped her little hand into Emily's.

"Will you sit next to me?" she asked.

"Of course," Emily said, giving her hand a squeeze.

"I like you," Margaret said, her voice just above a whisper.

"Well, I like you too," Emily replied, her heart breaking

anew at the fact that she would have to leave the girl, but not seeing any way around it.

"You speak to me as though I'm an adult, and," Margaret looked around her, as though to ensure no one could hear the two of them, "since you have come, Father has been quite pleasant toward me. I think he may actually be growing to like me some."

"Oh, Margaret," Emily said, stopping and crouching down beside her now, "your father has always liked you. In fact, he has always loved you very much."

"That's not what Mother said."

Emily bit her lip as she tried to find the right words, to assure the girl of her father's love without destroying her mother's memory.

"Sometimes," she began, "people do not quite understand one another. When that happens, they assume something to be true, when it's really not. Your mother and father may not have lived together as a married couple usually does, but your father always loved you. He just wasn't sure the best way to see you when you were still with your mother. After your mother passed, he thought you preferred that he wasn't near you. The only difference I have made, perhaps, is to help him find the right words to tell you how he thinks and feels."

Margaret nodded, her eyes, slightly teary now, wise beyond her years.

"I suppose that makes some sense."

"Good," Emily said with relief as she wrapped her arms around Margaret, pulling her close, wondering as she did when she had last been embraced. "Now, what do you say we go see that Yule Log? It's one of my favorite Christmas traditions."

Margaret's eyes were wide in her face when they entered the drawing room.

"I've never seen a Yule Log so large!" she whispered to Emily, who grinned at her.

"That is because I have not been here to select it," she responded with a wink. "I'm rather an expert on choosing one, you know."

She caught Charles' eyes, which gleamed at her words. At the reminder of all that had occurred following their search, Emily's cheeks began to warm, and soon the fire spread down through her body and out the very tips of her toes.

She cleared her throat.

"Is everything prepared?"

"Toller?" Charles said by way of response, and the butler appeared with a tray for Charles. He picked up a pitcher of what appeared to be oil and mulled wine, and they began to sprinkle it over the log as the family gathered around the hearth.

"Now," Charles said, holding up wooden splinters. "I have heard that in some households, it is the responsibility of a young girl to light the Yule Log from tinders of the log from last year."

He looked around the room as though in search of something — or someone.

"Now, wherever could I find a young girl?"

Margaret looked up at Emily as though asking if this was what she should take part in. Emily nodded in encouragement before she took her hand once more and walked with her to the front of the room where Charles awaited.

"Ah!" he said with feigned surprise. "Two beautiful women. Would one of them be able to help me light this?"

"I think Margaret may be best for the job," Emily said,

squeezing Margaret's shoulders for a moment before setting her free to go to Charles.

Margaret nodded, reaching out a slim hand to take the tinder. As she held it, Charles set the tip of the wood on fire, meeting Margaret's eye as he did so. For a moment, the two of them shared the smallest of smiles, and Emily's heart felt as though it had grown three sizes and was about to burst in two. She did, however, manage to keep from emitting any sort of exclamation.

Margaret brought the small tinders to the log, which, now covered in oil and wine, quickly caught fire. She stepped back as the flames began to dance in front of them.

"Now we give the log all of our bad tidings from the past year so that we can start afresh next year," Emily said, and she and Margaret closed their eyes to do so. When she opened them, she found that there were six pairs of eyes looking at her quite strangely.

"That is not... a tradition you follow?" she asked weakly, and they all shook their heads at her.

"As a matter of fact," Leticia said, "that is a tradition most often followed by country folk, I think."

"Perhaps it is," Emily replied, attempting nonchalance. "But I like the tradition. It seems appropriate for Christmastide."

The rest of them didn't seem appeased with her explanation nor inclined to join in, so Emily stepped forward with Margaret holding her hand, and silently mouthed what she wished to say. That she was going to throw away her fanciful ideas about any attraction or thoughts of a future with Charles. This evening was the perfect reminder for yet another reason of why they would never truly be together. His family already looked down upon her. Imagine if they knew the truth. She would focus on Charles' daughter instead. A thought entered her mind. Her sister was looking for a new placement as a governess. Perhaps this could be a good fit.

Emily took a deep breath. In with the new. A woman who would look after her parents with extra money. Who would go back to her position with Lord and Lady Coningsby and be the best governess one could be. And all would be well.

So why was the thought so melancholic?

16

Dinner was rather tedious, and Charles was grateful that Emily had been teaching the art of table manners long enough that her own were passable for it seemed that she was deeply scrutinized throughout the five-course meal.

She had insisted that Margaret eat with them — it was Christmas Eve, after all, she told them — and so she kept her attention on the girl, though Charles was surprised that she was genuinely attempting to make polite conversation with his family.

As soon as the meal was over, both Emily and Margaret left for bed, claiming exhaustion, and he only wished that he could follow.

"I must say, Charles," Edward said, strolling over toward him with a drink in hand after the meal, "I am surprised by your Mrs. Nicholls."

"And why would that be?" he asked, refusing to allow his cousin to rattle him.

"I wasn't sure that she was all that she seemed. In fact, as amusing as the thought is, I rather thought that you had randomly picked her out of a crowd!"

Charles attempted a chuckle. "That would be ridiculous."

"Maybe so," Edward said, looking closely at him. "And when will your nuptials be held?"

"We are still determining that," Charles said. "Perhaps this summer."

"This summer!" Edward exclaimed. "That is some time away. Why, with a woman of her age, you should be getting to things much more quickly, should you not?"

"Do not be crude, Edward," Charles said, casting a warning glare toward his cousin.

"Just saying, old man," Edward said with a chuckle. "But then, perhaps you do not require an heir, knowing your estate will be in safe hands with us. Well, it was a long, cold day of travel for us, so I'd best find my wife. Goodnight, Charles."

"Goodnight, Edward," he muttered, then left to find his own bed, grateful that at least one day with his family was done.

CHARLES WOKE RATHER EARLY the next morning, as light filtered into the room from behind his closed curtains. He rose, tucked his wrapper around himself, and crossed to the windows, opening them to find a fresh layer of pristine white topping the blanket of snow that covered the expansive grounds. It seemed yesterday's storm was holding.

He looked out over the rolling hills, noting smoke from his tenants' chimneys filling the air far below. A great weight of both power and responsibility descended on his shoulders as he looked out over the cottages dotting the landscape before him. This was his, for as long as he remained alive. After that... it would belong to Edward or Thaddeus if he didn't do something about it.

And yet he couldn't help the sense of excitement that filled him knowing that Emily slept just down the hall, that he would see her in a few hours' time. That he would be spending Christmas, her favorite time of year, with her. It was an honor, in a strange way, and one that he wasn't sure he deserved.

He rang for his valet and tolerated the man's impeccable ministrations as he dressed him for the morning. With his attire in order and his cravat properly tied, he hurried from his chambers and down the staircase.

"Good morning," he greeted Emily, pleased to find her the sole occupant of the dining room at the moment.

"Good morning," she said, smiling at him in return. Suddenly he felt like a young schoolboy greeting the object of his affection, and he hardly knew what to say. He filled his plate in the silence, sitting down next to her at the head of the large table.

"How are you today?" he asked, wishing that words came easier to him, that he knew exactly how to charm and woo a woman. He had never needed to, however. His marriage to Miriam had practically been arranged, and despite the fact that she had hated him and was hardly ever in the same location as him, let alone in his bed, he had been faithful. He had felt that he owed her that much.

After her death, he had far too much else to focus on and no desire to be caught in a liaison from which he could not easily extricate himself.

"I am well," she said with a small smile. "Happy Christmas, Charles."

"Happy Christmas to you, too," he said, enjoying the warmth her sherry eyes infused within his soul. "I do hope you enjoy spending the day with us."

"I will, I'm sure," she said, looking down at her plate so that all he could see was the top of her spectacles.

"When we lit the Yule Log yesterday, did you wish for anything?" she asked, but then immediately shook her head. "I'm sorry, please don't answer that. I shouldn't have asked. I was just curious."

He smiled, glad that he was not the only one slightly nervous following their time together.

"It's fine," he said, but then grew silent as he considered what to tell her, finally settling on the truth. "I wished that there was a way for me to pass on my title to someone other than Edward or Thaddeus. That I could look after all of the people who rely on me while still being able to... live life as I would choose."

He left unspoken the words of whether or not that life would include her. They hardly knew each other. And yet...

"You still have plenty of time to find a woman who can bear you a child," Emily said, and Charles wondered whether he correctly heard the hurt in her voice, or if it was simply part of his imaginings.

"I suppose so," he said, picking at the food on his plate, finding himself relieved when he heard footsteps behind them in the doorway.

"Margaret!" he exclaimed when his daughter walked in. "Happy Christmas."

She looked up at him with her wide blue-green eyes, and for a moment, he thought they were going to flick away from him as they always did, perhaps seek out Emily instead. But she held his gaze and after a moment of hesitation responded, "Happy Christmas, Father."

Charles' breath caught in his throat at her words, his eyes catching Emily's for a moment. He saw tears forming within them as a smile stretched across her face.

She nodded at him encouragingly and he cleared his throat before speaking once more.

"Did you sleep well?"

"I did."

"I have something for you," he said, reaching into his pocket and pulling out a small box. He had given her Christmas gifts before, but always through Miriam. He wondered now whether any of them had actually found their way into her hands, and if they had, who Miriam had given the credit to.

"What is it?" she asked, but he shook his head, refusing to answer her.

"Open it," Emily encouraged, and then Charles reached into his other pocket and passed a box over to her.

"And one for you."

"For me?" she questioned, her brow creasing, and he nodded, pleased to see the excited gleam in her eyes.

She looked over at Margaret. "Shall we open them together?"

The girl nodded and Charles saw them share a small smile of anticipation. They opened the boxes together, gasping in near unison at what was within.

"Oh, Charles!" Emily exclaimed. "This is far too much. I cannot accept this."

He reached into the box and picked up the necklace before rising from his chair and coming around behind her to fasten it around her neck. His fingertips skimmed her smooth skin as he did so. It would be so easy to succumb to the temptation to linger there, just for a moment, to—

"That's beautiful, Mrs. Nicholls," Margaret breathed as

Emily's fingers came up to brush the smooth red stones that were now fastened at her throat.

Margaret lifted her own necklace out of the box. It matched Emily's, but the stones were emeralds rather than rubies.

"It may not be, ah, appropriate for you to wear now," Charles said, wishing that Margaret would look at him to show him her thoughts regarding the gift, "but one day it will look quite beautiful on you."

He took the necklace from Margaret. "May I?"

She nodded, and he fastened her necklace for her, allowing it to then drift back down upon her shoulders.

"They were my mother's," he said, uncomfortable with how the two females were looking at him, as though he had given them each their own estate or something of the sort. "I wanted you both to have them so that you would always remember this Christmas together."

"These were in the trunk," Margaret said, her eyes wide, and then she clapped a hand over her mouth. "I'm sorry, Father, I looked in the trunk one time in your bedchamber. I—"

Charles placed a hand over hers.

"It's fine, Margaret. I'm glad you saw her things."

A smile larger than any he had ever seen her wear grew upon her face. "Thank you, Father. I can hardly wait for more Christmases in which all of us will be together."

Her words sobered both him and Emily, though she was much quicker to recover.

"We are fortunate to have this year," she finally said, and just in time as Lady Bishop and her husband chose that moment to walk into the room.

"My goodness!" his cousin Anita said, her gaze flitting

between Emily and Margaret. "Have you been raiding someone's jewelry box?"

"They were a gift," Charles said, his words somewhat biting, but he wanted his family to understand that they were not to question anything regarding Emily or Margaret.

Anita nodded quickly, sensing how serious he was, before her siblings and their spouses soon joined the room.

"We shall see you all after your breakfast. Perhaps some games in the saloon before the church service?" Charles said, motioning Emily and Margaret to accompany him out of the room, both of them looking relieved as they did so.

"Are we really going to play games, Father?" Margaret asked, and he looked over to Emily, who nodded encouragingly.

"Yes, I suppose we can, if Mrs. Nicholls has an idea of *what* we can play?"

"Games are one of my specialties," she said with a knowing smile. "My favorites at Christmas are charades or snapdragon, or even blind man's bluff."

"I've never played any of those," Margaret said, and Charles nodded.

"It's been some time since I have myself."

"Then we'd best play!" Emily exclaimed. "Come, Margaret, let's practice."

"I shall join in shortly, I promise," Charles said, watching them go, then nearly jumped in surprise when he found Toller was behind him.

"She's good for this household," Toller noted, surprising Charles with his forwardness, but he slowly nodded in agreement.

"Yes," he said, looking after her, "yes, she certainly is."

An hour later, he found his family members looking at

him as though he had gone mad when he held out a scarf for one of them to wear.

"Whatever is that for?" Leticia said, and he looked down at her.

"For the game," he explained. "For whoever is 'it'."

Leticia looked over at Emily, her eyes heavy with suspicion, as though she knew that she was the source of the game, but she sighed. "As long as it is not me," she said, lifting a hand to her hair. "It would ruin my hairstyle that took my maid hours."

Time not particularly well spent, Charles thought, but he was wiser than to comment upon it.

"Who shall be it?" Emily asked, and Edward was nominated by the rest of the party. Charles attempted to tamp down his jealousy when Emily had to touch Edward's shoulders in order to spin him around three times before she quickly joined the rest of the party in scampering away. Though he did find it rather comical to watch his cousin flounder around the room seeking out the rest of them. Edward had been far too interested in Miriam, and Charles had no wish to see another of his women succumb to his charms, though he hoped, this time, Emily would know better. She certainly didn't *seem* to be much inclined to enjoy Edward's attention. Perhaps because she had a chance to see the man he really was upon their first meeting.

Edward caught his son, who did not look pleased to have his father's hands on his face and hair as Edward attempted to figure out just who he had managed to capture, but when it was Thaddeus' turn, he was enthusiastic in his attempts to find another to take on the role, though Charles had to wonder whether he was peeking when he found Emily before any other.

She took the blindfold, not caring about her hairstyle as

she tied it around her head. His family took great delight in running from her, and Charles took the opportunity to watch her without her being able to witness him doing so. He had never met a woman like her. She didn't have the grace of a woman who was born into the aristocracy, nor the polished charm. Her charm, rather, was authentic, unique, and one that appealed to him more than any woman's ever had.

Damn it, he was falling in love with her. And he had no idea what to do about it.

As he stood there, shocked with the realization, her cool hands suddenly caught him from behind, as he had been so lost in his reveries he had failed to notice where she was.

"I say!" Edward called. "That is cheating, man. You practically waited for her to find you."

He grinned at Edward as Emily's hands began to wander over his face, for she had to determine just who she had captured.

"Charles," she said, her voice practically breathless, and he stood there with her hands upon him, looking down at her blindfolded face. Suddenly he was filled with thoughts of just what else he could do with her eyes covered so, and he reached his hands out to bring her closer toward him. He ran them up her arms, to the top of the cap sleeves of her morning dress, and he heard her suck in a breath as he brought them closer to her neck. He forgot everyone in the room, where they were, the time of day, the fact that all eyes were upon them as he leaned in to—

"Ahem," Edward said from behind him, and Charles turned around to look at him with a raised eyebrow. He *was* the earl, and damn it, if he wanted to kiss his betrothed in front of the lot of them, then he would very well do so. But then he caught Margaret's eyes upon him. The look on her face was one of exhilarated joy — and he realized belatedly that all he was doing was raising her expectations for something that would never actually come to pass.

Instead, he reached behind Emily and untied the blindfold.

"I suppose I'm it," he said, before taking off after Margaret, enveloping her in a tight embrace when he captured her and she squealed in glee.

As he held his daughter in his arms, all he could think was that perhaps there was something to Emily's Christmas after all.

17

Emily nervously looked at her reflection in the long mirror before her. The crimson dress hugged her curves, and she was not one who typically accentuated any of the voluptuous parts of herself, for she felt they were rather *too* voluptuous. She was curvy in all of the places men usually enjoyed — the bodice and hips — but she also had a bit extra in her stomach and her bottom that she could do without.

Fortunately, the style of the day ensured that the dress flowed out enough to cover some of the bits she didn't want on display, but still...

"You look wonderful, Mrs. Nicholls," Jenny said as she finished fastening the last of the buttons down Emily's back. Margaret nodded enthusiastically from her position on the bed, as she had insisted on being present while Emily prepared herself for the church service and the dinner to follow.

"Yes," Margaret sighed. "I wish I could be as beautiful as you someday."

"Oh, Margaret," Emily said, crouching down beside her, "you will be the most beautiful woman to ever be beheld."

Her words were true. With long, luxurious dark hair so like her father's and those aquamarine eyes, she would be a beauty that would break many hearts one day, that was for certain.

"Thank you, Jenny," she said to her maid before turning back to Margaret.

"Come, let's go join the others," she said, holding out her hand. "The church service will begin soon."

Emily breathed deeply as they continued along the curved corridor to the drawing room, attempting to slow her rapidly beating heart. She had been to many a Christmas service and had already met this family. What did she have to be nervous about?

Then they turned the corner and entered the drawing room, and she knew.

Her eyes immediately flew to Charles, catching sight of him standing near the fireplace. As they entered, he raised his head ever so slowly, his gaze arresting upon her where she and Margaret stood in the entryway. Emily couldn't have said who else was in the room at that moment, for it was as though there was a tether connecting her with Charles, and nothing and no one could break it.

He set his drink on the side table next to him, his eyes never leaving hers as he crossed the room toward them. He came to a stop a foot in front of them, and he lifted her hands to his lips, kissing each of them in turn.

Emily had never felt like such a lady as she did at that moment.

After one last long, lingering shared smile, Charles crouched down in front of the girl beside Emily. He took her hand in his and brought it to his lips as well, placing a quick kiss upon it.

"Lady Margaret," he said softly, "you look ever so lovely this evening."

"Thank you, Father," she said, her voice just above a whisper.

The entire moment was magical, and with all of her being, Emily longed for the three of them to remain in this small bubble of Christmas forever.

"You look rather fetching, Mrs. Nicholls," Mrs. Blythe said, coming over and perusing Emily from top to toe and back as though she was nothing more than a figurine upon which a dress was on display. "That dress is gorgeous. Isn't it, Katrina?"

"Oh yes, Mrs. Blythe," Lady Fredericton said as she joined her sister-in-law, "that color is quite lovely. Very rich."

She reached out and fingered the sleeve of the dress as though Emily wasn't even there.

Emily cleared her throat and retracted her arm.

"Thank you very much," she said with a polite smile, and the women finally met her eyes. "Both of you look quite beautiful this evening as well."

Their gowns were very elegant — and rather extravagant as well. They wore varying shades of pink, with flowers and jewels decorating intricate hairstyles.

Emily finally looked around the room, only to see that she had become the center of attention. Even Lord Bishop and Lord Fredericton, typically more focused on what was in their glasses and on their plates, were scrutinizing her, and she didn't much like it.

"Is it time to go?" she asked Charles, who wore a frown that mirrored what she was feeling at the moment.

"I think we'd better," he said, as the lot of them began to organize themselves for the journey to the church.

Despite the chill that clung stubbornly to the air, a warm flush filled Emily throughout the night. The party packed into two sleighs, and tucked in under the warm blankets next to Charles, she was acutely aware of his hard, muscled thigh pressed up against hers, of the frost in the air his breath was making just inches away, and of his right hand, which covered hers possessively. While she couldn't feel his warmth through the thickness of their gloves, she could sense by the pressure he placed upon her that he was feeling something of the same amount of connection that she was.

And in the church, when his gaze caught hers and they shared a smile, the Christmas spirit that had flowed through her very soul every year since she was a girl returned in spades.

"Happy Christmas," he whispered as the strains of *Adeste Fideles* filled the air. As Emily looked over at baby Jesus lying in the manger at the front of the church, she closed her eyes and prayed for a miracle.

CHARLES HADN'T BEEN able to focus on anything but Emily. The sparkle that seemed to always brighten her eyes had exploded tonight, her radiance as bright as the multitude of candles that lined the church around them. Her crimson dress accentuated her in all of the right places, and tendrils of her hair curled around her forehead, softening her face beautifully.

Charles knew he was continuing to act the lovesick pup,

yet he couldn't help but keep his gaze upon her during the church service, knowing that, at least to the eyes of all around him, she was his.

And so it was that his feet seemed to move of their own accord as he snuck through the family corridor later that night, as though he were a young man having a secret liaison with the forbidden daughter of a family friend and not the thirty-six-year-old earl who owned this entire estate meeting his betrothed.

Still, when he knocked gently on the door of her room while casting furtive glances around him, the secrecy of his actions only caused his heart to beat even faster.

She opened the door but a crack, through which he could see that she had already undressed for the night, a soft, worn pink wrapper closed tightly around her body, her hair cascading down around her shoulders in sandy waves.

"Charles," she said tentatively, opening the door wider to allow him entrance. "It's late."

"It is." They had played more games with his family following the service and dinner, Emily having proven herself rather adept at charades, but then, what did she not seem to excel at? "I have something for you."

She sat down on the edge of the bed while he perched on the stool in front of her vanity, turning it around so he was facing her.

"You have already been more than generous, in many ways. In fact, I cannot take the generous gift of your mother's jewelry. It wouldn't be right," she said, clasping her hands in her lap. "There is no need to give me anything else."

"The necklace is yours. I want you to have it," he said softly, running a hand through his hair nervously. He hoped she would appreciate his efforts, that she wouldn't think he was here to make love to her once more, though he longed to do so with all in his being. "This isn't much of anything. But I remember you telling me that your family would often make mistletoe together, even though your only purpose was to avoid it."

He had been holding his gift behind him since he entered, and he pulled it out now from behind his back.

"I asked Margaret to help me make this for you," he said, looking down at the ball of greenery in front of him. His efforts had been rather shoddy, but he hoped she would nonetheless appreciate them.

"I must apologize, for it's not exactly pleasing to look at, but—"

"It's perfect," she said, standing from the bed and walking over to him, lifting the ball of mistletoe from his hands as she inspected it before holding it close to her chest. "There could never be one that meant more to me than that which you and Margaret made together."

"Good," he said, inordinately pleased.

"When did you have time to do such a thing?" she asked.

"While you were preparing for the church service, we had a fair bit of time," he said with a teasing smile. "I could hardly believe how long it took!"

"I know," she said apologetically. "Never in my life has it taken me such time and effort to—"

"I'm teasing," he said, standing in front of her. "The attention was well worth it. You looked beautiful."

"Thank you," she said softly.

"Now, there is a reason I brought this to you tonight — alone."

"Oh?" she looked up at him, the expression in her eyes

almost coy from behind her lashes, though he knew it wasn't practiced. Emily was nothing but sincere.

"I thought perhaps we could see what would happen," he lifted the mistletoe over their heads, "if the two of us stood together beneath it?"

He could practically see the argument within her mind as it played out over her face — longing, frustration, pleasure, and doubt — but finally she sighed and took a step closer to him.

"I never could resist mistletoe," she said almost begrudgingly.

Before she could change her mind, he leaned down and captured her mouth with his, tasting her as though he were a man who had been deprived of drink for ages and was now finally able to quench his thirst.

He had come here to claim his kiss, and now that he started, he didn't know if he would ever be able to stop. How could he quit her, how could he leave her once all of this was over?

He couldn't. He wouldn't.

He could picture in his mind the family the three of them would become. Margaret was as enraptured by her as he was. All it had taken was a mention of a gift for Emily to have her agree to spend time alone with him that afternoon. And it seemed Emily was just as taken with Margaret. He couldn't let her leave them — she was what the two of them had needed in order to bring them back together and become a true family. If she left, then all would be lost.

Somehow, he had found himself on a different path than that which he had started upon, and he didn't think he would ever find his way forward.

"Emily," he murmured against her mouth, those lips that called to him, that begged him to taste them again. They were spicy, they were sweet, they were everything a man could ever want upon a woman's lips. He heard the swift intake of breath when he swept his tongue inside her mouth, his hunger for her insatiable.

She leaned back from him for but a moment.

"I've never had a kiss like this beneath the mistletoe before," she said, her breath coming quickly.

"I'd rather you said you never had a kiss like this... at all."

A delicate rosy hue blossomed across her cheeks.

"I haven't."

"Now you're only saying that because you know it's what I want to hear," he said, though with a smile, and she shook her head.

"I've always had a propensity to tell the truth," she said with a shrug. "It's a rather bad habit, I'm afraid."

"One that I don't overly mind," he countered. "So tell me this — is this the ugliest mistletoe you've ever seen in your life?"

"I've seen worse."

"Truly?"

"All right, I've seen only one worse than this. Most have... better composition, I suppose you can say. But this was obviously quite carefully made. And not only that, it has proven quite effective."

"Would you have kissed me without it?"

"Yes."

He grinned wolfishly at her. "I have to tell you, Emily, you make me feel like I can be myself. That I can set aside all of the ledgers and the responsibility, actually *enjoy* each moment for what it is. My daughter finally looks at me as though I am a human being and not a monster come to steal her away. I have you to thank for all of that."

She smiled shyly. "You're welcome."

He kissed her again, but this time his lips strayed, lightly feathering her forehead, her cheekbones, her nose, until he was nuzzling her neck and her arm curled around his shoulders to bring him closer toward her.

"Will you make love to me again?" she breathed, and he thought he might turn to liquid and melt into a puddle at her feet.

"That is not at all why I came," he murmured, though his body was yelling at him not to be a fool and to simply do as she said.

"You don't want me?"

"Of *course* I want you," he countered. "There isn't anything else I want as desperately. But I do not want you to feel beholden to do so."

"I am not asking you because I feel I should," she said indignantly, poking him in the chest. "I'm asking you because I want you, Charles Blythe. Despite the cold armor you raise in front of yourself, I have been witness to the man who resides underneath, the man with passionate fire hiding deep inside of him."

He chuckled ruefully as he wove his fingers through the silken tresses of her hair, spreading them down around her shoulders, winding a strand around his finger. How could hair the color of straw have the texture of the finest of satins?

"If that is what you want, love, then that is what you shall get."

This time when he took her lips, it was not lightly or softly, but with the fiery passion she had described. What she didn't know, what she couldn't know, was that there wasn't some strange being residing within him. She brought this out in him, showed him the man he never knew he could be.

And now the beast within him was coming out.

"Are you warm?" he asked between kisses.

"Warm?" she said breathlessly.

"Yes," he replied. "Perhaps it's time to lose your wrapper."

He pushed it off her shoulders until it was lying at their feet, and he lifted her slightly off the floor over top of it, backing her up toward the bed slowly, kiss by kiss.

He ran his hands up and down her arms, until she pushed hers into the front of his wrapper, and soon it joined hers on the floor. He wore only a nightshirt underneath, and when she ran her hands over it, apparently intrigued, he nipped her lip to distract her, bringing her back to the moment at hand as he dispensed of it entirely.

But then she was tracing the lines of his chest muscles, her fingers dancing over the hairs that dusted overtop it. When they glided over his nipples, stirrings within him that had long been dormant jumped to life, and he stroked his hands down her back to grip her bottom and pull her tight against him.

Without anything but the light, airy fabric of her night rail between them, the desire that had been threatening to explode finally did so. The air was filled with her — the rosewater she bathed in, the slightest muskiness of her skin, the essence of *her*. He backed her up toward the bed, and she scooted backward upon it until he was crawling on it and over her like a tiger hunting its prey.

This was so far from the obligatory couplings he had shared with Miriam that he didn't think he could have even called it the same act. This was more than sexual relations.

This was making love, of treasuring one another in more ways than he would have thought possible.

He found her nub of pleasure, teasing her, stroking her, until her legs opened of their own accord, inviting him in. He bunched her night rail in his hand as he lifted it to her waist, and when he buried himself inside of her, it was though he had come home.

Home, where he never again wanted to leave.

18

Emily had spent much of her widowed life within a nobleman's estate as a governess. Not quite a servant, yet not quite part of the family either.

Now, she was being treated like the lady of the manor, yet still not quite family — though she wasn't sure this family was one she would choose to be a part of in any case.

But then there was Charles. It was like she was in on a secret shared only by the two of them — for as reserved as he was all day long, at night, when he came to her, he was another man entirely.

It was four days past Christmas, and though it was still days away, Emily was anticipating the removal of Charles' cousins as eagerly as she was dreading the idea of being separated from Charles and Margaret.

"I can hardly believe that I never wanted to come here," she murmured to Charles as they danced together one evening. They had gathered in the saloon and Margaret was doing an admirable job of playing for them. She seemed to enjoy playing waltzes, for it was the second one in as many dances. Charles had claimed her hand for both of them, telling her that he would prefer to scandalize his cousins than to have to dance with any of them.

"Are you admitting that you had no desire to be in my company?" he responded to her with a raised eyebrow, one side of his lips turned up in a smile.

"I am admitting only that I was looking forward to Christmas at home with my family until you approached with another idea," she said, smiling innocently. "One that I should have turned down, but now I must admit that I'm rather happy I didn't."

"Because of my company?" he asked, his face remaining impassive, though his words had a teasing edge to them. "Or because of the… experiences we have shared?"

"You're impossible," she said, rolling her eyes, and he laughed.

She loved the loud, rolling sound of his laughter. It always began as a rumble deep in his chest before it seemed to bubble over out of his mouth, into the air to touch her soul. He didn't laugh often, but when he did, it filled her with joy.

"Apparently not wholly impossible," he said, "for you have actually made me *feel* again."

They locked eyes, and while their teasing filled the air between them, Emily was well aware of the deeper connection that lurked beneath the surface, one that neither of them wanted to address, for it was likely to only end in sorrow.

The music came to a close, and when an "ahem" sounded from beside them, they both turned to find Edward in wait.

"If you can find it in you to give another a turn, Charles, I would enjoy a dance with your Mrs. Nicholls."

"Of course," Charles said, though he seemed to relax

slightly when Margaret announced that she would play a quadrille.

Charles partnered Leticia, and the four couples formed a square as the dance began. Emily attempted to concentrate on Edward's words as she reminded herself of the steps, as it had been some time since she had taken part in such a dance herself.

"Tell us more about you, Mrs. Nicholls," Edward said as the two of them faced one another. "From where did you come?"

"*Chassés jetté, assemblé*," Emily muttered the steps to herself as they advanced toward Charles and Leticia.

Charles winked at her when they gave one another their right hands as they passed each other and then Edward took her left.

Emily managed, "From Newport," before they repeated the steps back the other way.

As they turned to face one another, Edward had another question ready and waiting.

"What is your father's profession?"

"*Balancé. Sissone Balotté, Assemblé*," Emily muttered and then raised her voice slightly so that he could hear her.

"He was a barrister."

Two-hand turn around one another to the left. Now that he was closer, Edward was truly focused on her.

"You were married?"

"I was."

"What happened?"

"He died."

"What was his profession?"

"A barrister as well."

"How did you meet Charles?"

Emily was grateful that it was now time for the *Chaine*

des Dames, so she had a moment to consider just what to say. She and Leticia passed one another in the center, giving each other their right hands, before she and Charles turned with one another, left hands pressed against each other.

"How did we meet?" she whispered to him.

"Pardon me?" he responded with wide eyes.

"We met at a ball," she decided as they turned once more. "It has to be the truth."

Recognition dawned in his eyes as he nodded, and then Emily was returned to Edward once more. As they turned with one another, she repeated her words.

"A ball," she said. "Charles and I met at a ball."

"When?" he asked as he took her hands in the promenade hold.

"*Chassés Jetté, Assemblé*," she repeated to herself three times. "Ah, recently," she said, hoping her forced smile would convince him.

"Well, if you are from Newport, I actually have some acquaintances from out that way," he said, his smile mirroring hers. "Perhaps you know them — Lord and Lady Rosthern?"

Emily was more than aware of them but she had no interest in continuing to discuss them.

"Perhaps," she said as the side couples began their dance. Goodness, how much longer would this take?

"Hopefully I'll know soon," he said jovially. "They could even attend your wedding!"

They certainly would not, Emily thought angrily, but then she recalled that she wouldn't actually be getting married. Not to Charles, nor to anyone else. She looked at him across the room, and he returned her gaze, though he wore a smile.

For the truth was, she could never marry anyone *but* him. And he had no interest in actually marrying her. He couldn't. And the fact that she completely understood exactly why not just made the entire situation much sadder.

"You are actually quite charming," Edward continued, "it must be why Charles likes you so much. I didn't quite understand it when he first introduced us, you know."

"Oh?" Emily said, though she had been more surprised than anyone that night in her employer's ballroom. "Because of its suddenness?

"No," Edward shook his head, but then changed the direction of the conversation — or so Emily thought.

"Have you ever seen a portrait of Miriam, Charles' first wife?"

"No, actually," Emily answered, now considering that it was somewhat strange. "I have not."

"Ah," Edward said with an all-knowing smile that made Emily shiver. "Come with me."

He held his arm out, and she reluctantly took it. He led her to the far wall of the saloon, where portraits and paintings extended so high they nearly touched the hands of the angels who danced along the ceiling.

The room was circular, covered in portraits, some of families, some of individual men and women who Emily assumed were previous earls and countesses. She hadn't paid any particular attention to them as there had been so much else with which to be occupied.

Edward led her over toward one of the sash windows, where one of the long velvet crimson curtains were drawn back, partially covering one of the portraits. He lifted it and Emily found herself staring into Charles' eyes, Margaret sitting on a chair in front of him, a solemn expression on her little face. She was young. Emily put her at five years old. And beside Charles was one of the most beautiful women Emily had ever seen. She had long, sleek dark hair, similar to that of both Margaret and Charles. Her eyes were a crystal blue that shone out of the portrait and right through Emily as though their bearer was still animate. She was tall, slim, and elegantly dressed. She looked as though she had been born to be painted into such a portrait.

"Wasn't she beautiful?" Edward asked with a sigh as he stared at the portrait. "This was Miriam. Charles' father may have chosen her, but Charles didn't argue once with he knew of her beauty."

Emily couldn't take her eyes off of her. After Charles had been married to a woman like this, how could he even consider being with someone like her?

No wonder they all seemed incredulous that Charles would betroth himself to her, with her spectacles and pudginess and, formerly, gowns that did her a disservice.

"She was very beautiful," Emily managed, agreeing with him.

"Yes, poor Charles to lose her so early," he said with a wistful shake of his head. "And poor Margaret, to lose her mother at such a young age. Well, we'd best be returning to the rest of them."

"Yes," Emily said, her voice just above a whisper. "We should."

CHARLES COULD HARDLY BELIEVE that he had met Emily just over a month ago, for it felt as though he had known her their entire lives. After the quadrille, Emily had taken over at the pianoforte, while he had partnered Margaret in a dance.

His daughter had been reluctant at first, but at Emily's

urging, she stepped into his arms and it felt to Charles as though his heart had leaped out of his chest and into hers.

He was returning to his bedchamber that night — where, after his valet assisted him, he would leave to join Emily — when he heard voices coming from the entrance of the corridor to the saloon. Thinking it was one of the servants, a smile came to his face in greeting, but he stopped abruptly in the doorway at the scene in front of him.

"Come, now, pretty one, just a little kiss. We are, after all, under the mistletoe."

"I— I thank you Mr. Thaddeus, but I've a man waiting for me, and I would hardly like to be disloyal—"

"He'll never know. No one will."

Thaddeus' arms came around the young maid, trapping her against the wall now as he leaned in, despite her attempts to squirm away.

"Thaddeus," Charles said in warning much more than greeting, and the man turned around at his voice. Charles expected him to push back away from the girl in embarrassment, but instead, he smiled even wider.

"Ah, Lord Doverton," he said. "I have to thank you for the mistletoe. It's already provided me plenty of fun."

"You should be ashamed of yourself," Charles scolded, knowing he was treating his nephew like Emily would one of her charges, but he hardly cared. He motioned to the girl to leave now that he had Thaddeus distracted, and the girl nodded and slipped out of Thaddeus' arms and down the hall as fast as she could. "I will not have you harassing my servants. You leave them alone for the remainder of your time here, do you hear me?"

"I am only availing myself of what will be mine one day," Thaddeus said with a smirk. "Are you feeling well these days, my lord? Or should I continue with my preparations?"

He began to chuckle as he left him and walked down the hall, his laugh echoing through Charles' very soul as he considered what the future would hold with Ravenport in Thaddeus' hands. It was the very reason he had told Edward he was marrying, why he had chosen a random woman from a crowd and announced her as his betrothed — to give himself some time until he found a woman who would likely provide him with a child.

When he closed his eyes to imagine a woman walking down the aisle toward him, a woman who would support his daughter, who would be in his bed night after night, who would walk with him around these very halls of Ravenport, there was only one face he saw. Emily's.

But if he married her, it would only be for himself. For he would be leaving Ravenport and all within and around it — his servants, his tenants — to the heir as well. How could he subject them to that misery, in order for himself to be happy?

He wouldn't. He couldn't, he realized as his heart seemed to tear in two, between Emily and all who relied on him.

He had to place some distance between them so that when it was time for her to leave, it wouldn't be nearly so painful — for him, or her.

Starting now.

"Hello, Charles," Emily said softly as she shut the door behind him. She had been waiting for him for so long that she was beginning to wonder whether or not he was even going to come. She hardly wanted to admit, even to herself, just how much she looked forward to his nightly visits. It wasn't even because of the love they made together. It was the fact that in these few hours, they could be alone together without pretense. She had thought that in this stolen time, Charles wanted her, Emily Nicholls, for no reason other than herself.

However now, after seeing Miriam, she questioned what Charles saw in her. What exactly did he want from her? Was it simply because she was conveniently here? Would it matter if she was any other woman?

It irked her to no end that she was questioning herself like this, but she couldn't keep the thoughts from entering her mind.

"My apologies. I know it is late," he said rather formally, stepping into the room, and when he looked around the chamber at everything *but* her, Emily's heart instantly dropped.

"What's wrong?" she asked softly, her palms beginning to sweat now.

"Nothing," he said quickly — too quickly — shaking his head. "Nothing at all. I just thought... well, I wanted to come to you so that you were not waiting for me, but there is something we must speak of."

He was silent for a moment before he finally met her eyes. "I think perhaps it's best that we no longer spend time together... in this way."

"In this way?" Emily repeated. Since her conversation with Edward, she had half-expected this, but still, it hurt more than she cared to admit. "You mean being intimate with one another?"

"Yes," he nodded, looking relieved that she had said the words instead of him. Emily had always been fairly candid, while she was sure that Charles had been raised to not put such things into words. "Since we are not married, and even more so, have no intentions to be, I am worried about potential consequences."

"We've had this discussion before," she sighed, sitting heavily on the bed, wondering at the fact that he would have forgotten what she had told him, since producing an heir seemed of such vital importance in his mind. "I am not likely to conceive so you needn't be worried."

"Even so," he said, looking rather uncomfortable, "this isn't fair for either of us."

His words were hurried, more uncertain than any she had ever heard from him. He was always so resolute.

"What happened?" Emily asked, sensing that something was amiss. "What changed?"

"Nothing," he said abruptly. "Nothing at all. My responsibilities remain as they always were. I was simply reminded of how remiss I have been in adhering to them. I should be going. Goodnight, Emily. I look forward to seeing you on the morrow."

And with that, he was gone, leaving Emily standing there staring at the door with her mouth wide open.

He had rejected her.

And as the knife pierced through her heart, it hurt more than she ever could have predicted.

19

"Mrs. Nicholls?"

Emily groaned inwardly as Edward cornered her on the way to the dining room. She looked up hurriedly to ensure there was no blasted mistletoe hanging above them, and then stopped and waited for him to join her.

"Yes, Mr. Blythe?" she said patiently, worried about the smug smile on his face as he began walking with her, their steps in time.

"Do you recall, a few days ago, when I mentioned some mutual acquaintances?"

"Yes..." she said, closing her eyes for a moment. She had hoped that their conversation was the last she had heard of Lord and Lady Rosthern, but this man was like a dog with a bone once he was onto something.

"Well, I wrote to them upon speaking with you here at Ravenport, asking them to send their return correspondence to me here. And wouldn't you know it, a letter arrived from them today."

Emily groaned inwardly, everything within her desiring

to turn around and flee from him, down the corridor to the safety of her room.

"It seems they *do* know your family," he said, his grin stretching wider to the point that it became almost demonic. "Lord Rosthern tells me that both you and your sister have enjoyed posts as *governesses*. And wouldn't you know it, your sister was more than friendly with Lord Rosthern. It seems that she desired a rather *close* relationship with him."

Emily stopped and whirled about, raising a finger and pointing it toward the horrid man. He could say what he wanted about her, but she would not listen to him disparage her sister.

"Let me make something abundantly clear, Mr. Blythe. There was no relationship between them at all outside of employer and governess. Lord Rosthern attempted to take advantage of my sister, which was why she left their employ. He may say otherwise, but it is nothing but a lie. You will not speak poorly of my sister when she did nothing but govern those children with their best interests at heart."

He laughed, its sound setting all of the hairs on Emily's arms on edge.

"Oh, you are quite the defender, Mrs. Nicholls," he said, raising a finger to stroke her cheek and she recoiled. "It is quite endearing. But never mind your sister. She is of little consequence to me. What is most intriguing is the fact that you work for Lord and Lady Coningsby. Tell me, do they know of your entanglement here with my good cousin? I find it hard to believe that you would continue in their employ were you engaged to marry Charles. A future countess would hardly need to continue as a governess. Tell me, at what ball did you happen to meet Charles? It wouldn't be the one at the Coningsby residence, now would it?"

Emily remained caught up in his words, frozen into silence at all he had surmised, the majority of it unfailingly true.

"I—" she began, attempting to find the words. "I am a governess, yes," she admitted, but held her head high, refusing to be ashamed. "But wh-what does that matter?"

"Oh, it matters Mrs. Nicholls," he said, advancing on her, and Emily took one step back for each one he took forward until she was flush against the wall. "It matters very much. I was always suspicious of this little ruse Charles created, naming you his betrothed. Now that I know the truth, once I tell others of it, Charles will be a laughingstock."

"It will make no difference," Emily said, squaring her shoulders, refusing to be cowed. "Charles is aware I am a governess, and he can marry me if he so chooses. I wouldn't be the first governess to become a lady. And if he— if he doesn't choose to marry me after all, then he will find another quite quickly, I am sure."

"Yes, but what good family would want to tie themselves to a man who would pretend to marry a woman and then drop her just as quickly — and a governess at that? All would know that you are truly nothing more than a mistress."

"I am *not* his mistress," Emily said, though the words sounded false even to her own ears.

"No?" Edward said, raising his eyebrows. "Then Charles truly is going to marry you?"

Emily was silent.

"If there is a scandal, Mrs. Nicholls, then it will take considerably more effort for Charles to marry. I'm sure he will in time — after all, he *is* an earl and there are many desperate young ladies. But Charles can hardly stand such social events as it is. If he is made a laughingstock? Ha, he'll never do it, and the title is as good as mine — or Thaddeus'. Unless..."

"Unless what?" Emily asked, a sick feeling filling her stomach, for she knew that no good was going to come of this conversation.

"Unless you leave," Edward said, eyeing her with a smirk. "Leave him, leave this house, be gone before the Twelfth Night celebration. Go back to your life, Mrs. Nicholls, your little family in Newport and your position as governess with the Coningsbys. Do so, and I will ensure the family keeps you a secret. We shall all forget this ever happened," he paused, "well, except you. I'm sure you will never forget being the potential wife of an earl for as long as you live."

He leaned in, and Emily could smell his vile breath as his mouth neared her face. He might resemble Charles in looks, but in every other way, they were as different as a lump of coal and the ruby in her necklace.

"Go home, Mrs. Nicholls. Pack your spectacles and your mistletoe, and leave behind your new gowns for those that belong on that figure of yours. Here."

He passed her a handful of coins, and Emily didn't even think as her hand opened of its own accord and he passed them over.

"That will be more than enough to pay for a stagecoach home. The roads should be cleared by now. Safe travels, Mrs. Nicholls."

And at that, he winked, turned on his heel with his hands behind his back, and continued down the hall, whistling a merry tune as he went.

~

CHARLES RUBBED HIS EYES WEARILY. It had been a long night, for he had hardly been able to sleep a wink. All he could picture was Emily's face, so hurt, so angry, as she stared at him following his dismissal of her after their nights together.

He was only trying to do right by her. He couldn't commit himself to her, not when so many others relied on him. He never should have become involved with her, but the truth, as difficult as it was to admit, was that he hadn't been able to help himself.

And now look at him.

There was one thing he *could* do, however. He could go speak with her once more, explaining himself much better this time. Surely then she would understand his reasoning and would know that his dismissal had nothing to do with her, but, in fact, was because of just how drawn to her he was.

Charles knocked lightly on the door of her chamber, though he wasn't surprised when she didn't answer. He opened the door ever so slightly to see within, but the room was dark, the space empty.

"Emily?" he called, but he instinctively knew she wouldn't be there. She must have already gone down for dinner. Charles turned to leave but then his eye caught a glint of red on the vanity table, where the large ruby stones reflected the setting winter sun shining through the window.

He walked over, his steps hurried, and there he found the necklace, sitting next to the mistletoe he had fashioned with his own hands.

Charles strode across the room, yanking open the doors

of the wardrobe. Dresses remained, but with a sick feeling in his stomach, he rifled through the layers of colorful silk, muslin, and satin. It was just as he had thought. No drab grays. No high-necked navy blues.

She had taken only that with which she had come.

She was gone.

∼

EMILY HURRIED THROUGH THE SNOW. She could catch the last stagecoach coming through Duxford if she rushed. In no time at all, she would be at her parents' house. First, however, she had to get through the two-foot-high piles of snow as the wind battered her face. It was slow going, but damned if she was going to stay at Ravenport for one more moment.

She had tried to fulfill her promise and do her duty, but she had failed.

She had failed because she had fallen in love with Charles. She knew she should have gone to him, should have told him what Edward knew and what he had threatened. But just last night Charles had ended anything between them himself, and she had finally come to the realization she should have on the day he had offered her this position.

Her pride, her love, was not worth any amount of money that he had to offer her. Yes, she could then pay to support her parents. But it was far better that she just redouble her efforts to save her wages for them. And, if nothing else, perhaps she could send her sister here to take on the duty of governess with Margaret.

Poor Margaret. The girl had sobbed when Emily had said goodbye to her — she didn't have it in her to leave without doing so — but Emily had promised to visit very soon. And visit she would. It was both a blessing and a curse that they were not far away. For as much as Emily would like to sever all ties if she must leave Charles, she would always have this connection to Margaret.

"I'm sorry," she had said to the girl, "but it's time for me to leave Ravenport."

"But you *love* him," Margaret had protested, and Emily's eyes filled with tears. Margaret was far more perceptive than Emily or Charles had realized.

"Which is the very reason I'm leaving," she had whispered in response. "Your father needs to find a woman who can be a true mother to you, who can give you brothers and sisters and all the happiness in the world." She had gathered Margaret's face in her hands. "But I promise you, I will visit, as often as I am able to. Your father loves you, very much. All you need to do is give him a little encouragement, and you'll find he will learn how to show you that he does."

Margaret nodded, wise beyond her years, and Emily's heart broke a little more.

"Write me a song, will you?" Emily had asked, and Margaret had nodded.

Oh, but she was going to miss that little girl. Emily began sniffing anew, but attempted to blink back the tears — it was so cold, they were likely to freeze to her face. Her attachment to Margaret, however, was all the more reason to leave sooner rather than later, for that was another connection that would only be harder to break the longer Emily stayed.

As Duxford came into her sight, Emily noticed the stagecoach parked outside of the postal office.

"Oh, dear," she said, hurrying her footsteps, her feet beginning to freeze as the snow wet through her boots. Why did it seem she was continually attempting to freeze herself to death as of late? She hated being cold. And yet cold now seemed to be her state of being far more often than she would like.

By the time Emily made it to the middle of the town, her cheeks were so frozen they felt near waxy to her touch, and her breath was a cloud around her head.

She passed her small bag to the coachman, who was bundled in so many layers that Emily nearly couldn't see his face.

"Where are you off to?"

"Newport," she managed.

"Ah, not far, then, just the next town," he said. "But it will be a bit of a wait. We've just stopped to warm up for a moment. Most of the others are in the tavern."

"Thank you," she said, hurrying in herself.

The tavern was located in the first floor of the inn but was nearly like being outdoors, for it seemed the entirety of it was covered in greenery. Christmas certainly hadn't been forgotten here.

Emily took a seat at a small two-person table over-looking the street through the window, the edges of it frosted over from the cold.

She ordered a warm chocolate when the innkeeper came over to ask what she might like, cupping her frozen hands around the mug once it arrived.

She had just taken her first sip when she noted a pair of beautiful horses coming up the road in front of the inn. They were attached to a handsome sleigh. She knew those horses, knew that sleigh.

The Earl of Doverton, she realized with a gasp as Charles stepped out of the sleigh and then hurried down and quickly conversed with the stagecoach driver before he began to stride toward the inn, his cloak billowing out around him, captured by the wind.

Whereas Emily's entrance into the tavern had nearly gone unnoticed, when Charles stepped through the creaky wooden door that was just slightly taller than he was, all heads turned toward him. He barely spared anyone else a glance, however, and Emily's heart jumped when his eyes met hers from across the room.

He had followed her. Did that mean— but no, he was simply worried, she read in his glance. He hastened toward her, as though concerned that she was going to run away — though she supposed that made sense, for she had already done so once today.

"Emily," he greeted her, his tone matter-of-fact as he sat down across from her, though he made no motion toward her for he was apparently afraid of a frosty reception. "You left."

"I had to."

"No, you didn't," he said urgently, shaking his head. "I did not mean to reject you, Emily. It's only—"

"I understand, truly I do," she responded, twining her fingers together in an effort to prevent them from reaching across the table toward his. "We were becoming far too close when I would be leaving anyway. I know I left earlier than promised, but I will not take the money from you."

"Take all the money you want, I do not care."

"I couldn't."

"You must."

Emily said nothing in response, for she had said all there was to say. She had spoken the truth. No matter what Edward had found out, no matter what he threatened, Emily knew she and Charles could face it together. But it would be far too difficult alone.

"Why... why didn't you say goodbye?" he asked, and Emily read the hurt in his normally stoic expression.

"Because," she said, her voice breaking, "it was too painful."

"It doesn't have to be," he said, reaching across the table and holding out his hands until she put hers within them. "Come back, Emily, please? We'll figure something out, I promise. I don't know what but all I know now is that I— I cannot lose you."

"What is there to determine?" she asked, a tear escaping her eye. "You need an heir, or else Thaddeus is going to inherit all. Can you live with that?"

Charles was silent, and Emily could tell he was struggling with the dilemma.

"It isn't fair to make you choose," she said softly, "so I will choose for you. Go home, Charles. Go home to Margaret, and be the very best father you can be for her. Find a bride," she swallowed a sob, "who can give you all you need, and provide you all the heirs you could ever want. I'll be fine."

She wouldn't be, but she couldn't tell him that.

"All here for the stagecoach, we're boarding!"

Emily looked up when the driver called for them, grateful for the interruption, and she began to rise.

"Farewell, Charles."

"Emily—"

"Please, Charles," she said desperately, "it will only make things worse."

"At least let me take you the rest of the way in the sleigh."

"I cannot let you do that," she said, for she could not spend one more moment with him or she might break and agree to do anything required to be with him. "Go home. Home to your family, to your daughter. And thank you."

"For what?" he asked, his voice gruff.

"For showing me what love truly feels like," she said, cupping his face in her palm for a moment before she turned, lifted her hood, and ran from the inn before the tears truly began to flow.

20

Charles was in a state of shock when he arrived back at Ravenport. His family tried to ask him where he had been and what had he done with Mrs. Nicholls, but he didn't bother to respond. Instead, he made his way to the music room, knowing better than to check the nursery. His daughter hardly seemed to even use the room he had created for her, with dollhouses and every toy a child could want.

Apparently, it didn't matter how many objects a parent gave a child if that parent did not also show her what affection truly was.

His daughter had never been an overly talkative child, but he now realized that it wasn't difficult to ascertain her feelings — one only had to listen to the music she played. As he neared the music room, he could hear the forlorn melody as it traveled out of her fingers, through the keys and down the curved corridor. It brought tears to his eyes, so accurately did it reflect his current emotions.

He didn't knock on the door until the last strains of the

minor chord dwindled and she sat for a moment, staring at the piano in front of her, with not a page of music to be seen.

"Margaret?" he said, entering the room only when she turned to acknowledge him.

"Father," she said softly, and he slowly eased himself into the chair across from the piano bench so that she could see him without turning. He longed to take her in his arms, to hold her so they could take comfort in one another, but he didn't know if she was yet ready.

"I'm sorry, Margaret," he said, leaning forward, his head in his hands at his somber little girl. She had been deprived of a childhood, he realized, and he could blame no one but himself.

"For what?" she asked softly.

"For everything. For bringing Emily here, for raising any hopes you might have had. I hadn't realized that she would be so..." he searched for the right word.

"Wonderful?"

"Yes, wonderful," he said with a sigh. "She truly is, isn't she?"

"She is, Father," Margaret said, looking down at her hands in her lap before she raised her sea-green eyes to his. "Do you love her as much as I do?"

"I do," he admitted.

"So why did you let her leave?"

"It's difficult to explain," he said slowly. "As you know, however, I won't always be here. This estate, the earldom and all it holds, will go to another. If it was just the building itself, or the land, I wouldn't be so concerned. But it's the people, Margaret. I cannot allow the servants and the tenants to be ruled by Edward or Thaddeus. They have no care for others, are only concerned for themselves. How could I be so selfish as to leave it all to them?"

"Why would they become earl?" she asked, with, he thought, the wide-eyed innocence of a child. "Would I not be the countess?"

Charles risked reaching out to run a hand over her sleek hair.

"Unfortunately, darling, that is not to be," he said with a sigh. "The title passes through the male line."

"No, it doesn't," she countered, looking at him as though he were daft.

"Well, yes," he said, trying to be gentle with his daughter. "That's just the way it is."

"No, it's not," she argued, becoming adamant now. "Grandfather said so."

"Grandfather?"

"Yes," she insisted. "And Mother too. They didn't want you to know."

"I think I would know of the inheritance of my own line," he said, cursing Miriam and her lies, but managed a smile for Margaret to ease his words.

"No, Grandfather ensured that you wouldn't know," she said, shaking her head and staring intently at him. "Mother said he always hated that fact that a female could inherit the earldom so he made sure to hide it from you. Mother discovered it one day when she was in his study and she asked him about it. He told her the truth, but made her swear she wouldn't tell you."

Charles nearly couldn't breathe, so overwhelmed he was with both the knowledge and the deception. All of this time, he had never known that his *daughter* could inherit?

"Your mother knew?" he asked Margaret as he finally caught his breath, and she nodded.

"She told me she didn't think it would be much of a life, to be a countess and have to worry about all of the responsibility that should be a man's, so she didn't want you to know either."

"I see," Charles said, lacing his fingers together and bringing his thumbs up to rest against his forehead. "And what do you think?"

He knew it was a lot to ask. She was only eight years old for goodness sake. And yet wise beyond her years.

"I think..." she said, rubbing at her forehead. "I think that if you taught me, I could do just as good a job as a man."

Charles grinned. "I think you could too. Let me look into this, all right?"

"Father," Margaret looked up at him, wise beyond her years. "Does this have something to do with Mrs. Nicholls? For even if I am wrong, you could very well live longer than anyone else who might inherit, or you could have a son with Mrs. Nicholls, could you not? You never know what will happen."

Charles could only stare at his daughter in wonderment. Eight years old, and yet it seemed she was filled with greater wisdom than a woman of advanced age.

For she was right. While he would do all he could to ensure his line continued with someone who would look after the title with all of the responsibility it required, he couldn't predict the future, nor completely control the fortunes of any of his family.

He took her hands in his.

"You make a very good point, my dear," he said. "Now, what do you say we go tell Mrs. Nicholls of all this?"

She nodded, dimples appearing in her cheeks.

"Very good," he said. "Now, let's go find your warmest cloak."

"EMILY!"

She hadn't even started up the walk when Teresa was running out of the door and down the street in just her gown, despite the cold. She wrapped Emily in an embrace warmer than any fire, and Emily dropped her bag to squeeze her back in equal measure.

"Oh, Emily, I missed you!"

"I missed you too!" Emily exclaimed, tears running down her face anew. Goodness, but she had cried more these past two days than she had in years.

"Christmas wasn't the same without you."

"Wait until you hear all about mine!"

"Girls!"

They turned to the voice of their mother from the doorway of the house. Emily laughed through the tears at her mother continuing to refer to them as girls despite the fact that they were both in their thirties.

"Come in before you catch a fever."

She was far past the point where she might make herself ill, but she wasn't about to tell her mother that, for she had enough to worry about already.

Her mother's embrace was as warm as her sister's, and soon they all had tears in their eyes.

"It's good to see you," her father said after limping over to the door, his white bristly beard brushing Emily's shoulder in the most reassuring way when he held her close.

No matter how old one was, Emily mused, nothing was like coming home to one's parents.

Scents of freshly baked bread, roasted meat, and fresh greenery wafted over Emily as she entered through the foyer. The fire in the grate was roaring, the table was set for dinner, and there, in the middle, was the plum pudding.

"We haven't cut into it yet," her mother said, following her gaze. "We were waiting for whenever you arrived."

"Oh, Mother. Thank you," Emily said with a watery smile. "Has James' family been here?"

"Yes, they celebrated with us on Christmas Day," her mother said. "They asked us to wish you Happy Christmas from them, and they hoped you would visit them once you arrived home."

"Good," Emily said with a smile, "and I will."

"Come, get changed now," her mother said, ushering her through the front room to the back bedrooms, where Emily knew her mother left their bedchamber intact for the times they would come home to visit. "Once you're freshened up, we'll get you a blanket and a warm plate. Then plum pudding it is."

Emily did as instructed, and soon found herself sitting in a plush upholstered chair in front of the fireplace, her parents and sister in their usual places around her. It was as though time stood still here in her parents' home.

Her mother brought her a warm cup of tea along with some of their dinner from earlier, then sat down across from her, pulling out her knitting needles and yarn. She sat back, but her posture didn't fool Emily. She looked her in the eye and said, "All right, out with it. What has happened?"

"Nothing," she said, attempting to set aside her cares so as to not worry her parents. But at her mother's probing stare, and with her sister's hand on her arm, she soon found herself pouring out the entire story — with a few omissions — as her family listened on with sympathetic stares.

"Oh, darling," her mother said, reaching out a hand and placing it on her knee. "I'm so sorry."

"It's my own fault," Emily said with a sigh. "I knew what the situation was ahead of time."

"So why did you do it?" Teresa asked, and Emily looked over at her inquisitive stare, wondering how to best answer that.

"Were you paid for it?" her father asked knowingly, and Emily nodded.

"I hope you didn't do it for us," he said before his words dissolved into coughing, and Emily started to say no, but she knew that her parents would see right through her, as they always did.

"I thought it wouldn't be a difficult task for the help it would provide us," she said, looking down. "How was I supposed to know that I would fall in love with the man?"

"It sounds as though he loves you in return," Teresa said gently. "Could he not put aside all of his worries for you, if that's how he truly feels?"

"He's too good a man for that," Emily said, hearing the melancholy in her voice. "He cares too much."

They were all silent for a moment but then jumped when there was a knock at the door.

"Who would that be?" Emily asked with a frown, looking around at her equally perplexed parents.

"I'll get it," her mother said, but her father raised his hand to stop her as he slowly rose from his chair.

"A man can answer his own door, Mary," he said, limping over to the door, and Emily shared a look with Teresa. Both his hip injury and his cough only seemed to be getting worse since a fall last year.

The door finally creaked open, and they all craned their necks to see who was behind it, but they couldn't see around Emily's father.

"Happy Christmas," they heard him say, but the rest of the exchange was muffled.

"Who could it be?" Teresa asked, and Emily shrugged in response.

"Emily?" her father said, turning around to face her. "Someone is here to see you."

"Oh?" Emily said, rising, the blanket falling away from her shoulders to rest on the chair.

Her heart stopped as in stepped Charles and Margaret.

21

"Charles?" Emily gasped, her body as frozen as it had been during their icy Yule Log search as she stood and stared at them. "What are the two of you doing here?"

Charles could see the confusion in her eyes, the internal battle waging within her over welcoming them and wishing he had never come. But none of that would matter in a moment.

He crossed from the foyer to the living room in a few quick steps, and before he could even think of what he was doing or consider that her entire family was witnessing the scene, he had her in his arms. He held her head against his shoulder as he clutched her tightly against him, closing his eyes as the scent of rosemary wafted up from her hair into his nostrils.

How could he have ever let her go? What a fool he was.

When he finally opened his eyes, the first thing he saw was Margaret looking up at him with a wide smile on her face. Then he realized that Emily's family members were all staring at him with bemused expressions, though he sensed they were accompanied by smiles of pleasure.

Finally, a woman who looked very much like Emily, only with a few more wrinkles and gray hair instead of hair the color of sand, took a step toward them.

"You must be Lord Doverton," she said with a warm smile. "Welcome to our home."

Charles reluctantly released Emily and gave the woman his hand.

"Thank you," he said, looking around the room at the lot of them. "Thank you very much and my apologies for the interruption."

He sought out Emily once more, finding her crouched down embracing Margaret. Of course. He would expect no less.

"Charles," she said, looking up at him with a somber expression, "while I am thrilled to see you here, do you truly believe this is the best course to take? We've discussed this, and—"

"Emily," he said, taking her hands and pulling her to her feet, "there is much to tell you. It seems that anything which would have stood in our way has disappeared."

"But—"

"The beautiful child standing before you is none other than the future Countess of Doverton."

Emily turned to look at Margaret, her chocolate brown eyes wide when they returned to Charles. "I don't understand."

"It seems that my father omitted some important details regarding the Doverton title. Our line is one of the very few in England that can be inherited by a son *or* a daughter should no sons arise."

"How is that possible?" she exclaimed, her fingers clenching his more tightly.

"Apparently there is a special remainder on the inheritance that *any* heir of the body can inherit — not just a male," Charles said. "At least, that is what I could surmise from the quick read I did of the letters in my study. They were buried so far back in the bookshelf I almost didn't find them. I cannot say I took particularly long to review them, as Margaret and I were quite eager to follow you."

"You were significantly quicker than the stagecoach, that is for certain," Emily said, as practical as always, though she still wore a look of confusion.

"Besides that," Charles said, squeezing her hands and looking deeply into her eyes so she would know just how serious he was about his next words, "I've finally realized that even if I am wrong, it doesn't matter."

"What are you talking about?" she demanded. "Of course it does."

"It doesn't," he said, shaking his head. "For so long I have been trying to control the future and the lives of more than just myself. But what I should have realized long ago is that there is so much *not* in my control. I married Miriam thinking that she would provide me with multiple heirs but it was not to be. Then she passed, which no one could ever have predicted. And then I met you and fell in love with you, which I certainly had not planned."

Her eyes widened significantly as he admitted his feelings. Her mouth opened and closed, but no sound came out.

"I cannot know what the future will hold," he continued. "Even if our assumptions prove wrong, we do not know whether you and I will ever have children together. We do not know if and when Edward would ever hold the title, nor if Thaddeus would even show any interest in living at

Ravenport or managing the estate himself. Perhaps he would simply sit in London as he already does and allow a hopefully competent steward to manage his affairs."

He looked around now, knowing he was explaining to all of them, as they were holding onto his words with rapt attention.

"There is, however, one thing I do have control over," he said urgently, imploring Emily to understand. "That is to marry the woman I love, to spend my life as happy as I could ever hope to be. And," he said, reaching a hand out to draw Margaret toward them, "I can be there for my daughter, showing her how much I love her. I can exemplify to her what love should look like between a husband and wife. And I can allow you, Emily, to be in her life as well."

He bent down on one knee in front of Emily, taking one of her hands in both of his.

"Emily Nicholls," he said, swallowing the lump in his throat, "you are the lovliest, most intelligent, thoughtful woman I have ever met. You are warm, kind, and caring, and you have shown me that life is more than duty and responsibility. I cannot say I will ever be the carefree spirit you likely deserve, but I will do my very best to make you happy for the rest of my life. Will you be my wife?"

Her smile was wide, her eyes watery, as she crouched down to take his face between her soft — freezing — palms.

"Yes, of course I will marry you, Charles," she said, which caused her sister to cheer and Margaret to jump up and down, displaying more emotion than Charles had ever seen from her.

His heart felt near to bursting as he picked up Emily, twirling her around before setting her down on her feet and taking her mouth in a long, promising kiss — one that was just chaste enough to be proper in front of his daughter and

Emily's family, but enough to remind her of all that lay between them and the future to come.

As he set her down, he caught her father's eye.

"That is to say — if it is all right with you, Mr. Nowell."

The man chuckled as he stroked his beard. "Of course it is, Lord Doverton."

"Charles."

"Charles, then. Welcome to the family."

"And you," Mrs. Nowell said, crouching down in front of Margaret, "look as though you could use some plum pudding. What do you say?"

"I believe that is an excellent idea," Margaret said in her small yet serious voice, and the rest of them laughed slightly.

"Come, come," Mrs. Nowell said, taking Margaret's hand and leading her toward the table, where she picked up the plum pudding from the center. "The rest of you sit while the two of us go prepare this."

As Mr. Nowell and Emily's sister followed them to the dining room, Charles took the moment with Emily all to himself to bestow another quick kiss on her lips as he wrapped his arms around her waist.

"Are you sure?" she questioned, her eyes searching his. "I am a widowed governess, Charles. Hardly the type of woman fit to become a countess."

"I think I am to be the judge of that," he said sternly. "You are everything I could ever ask for, Emily. Remember that."

"Very well," she said, a dimple appearing in her cheek. "I shall do as you say — in this regard, anyway."

He laughed then, tucking her hand in the crook of his elbow while leading her to the table as though he were escorting her through the most proper of balls. He held out her chair and helped her into it, taking the seat next to her just as Mrs. Nowell entered with Margaret at her side. The two of them held a platter featuring a large, speckled ball of plum pudding. A piece of holly sat on top, while around the pudding spectacularly blazed what Charles assumed was brandy.

The fire reflected in Margaret's eyes, which were dancing with excitement. Then she climbed on his lap, and Charles thought if his heart became anymore full, it might burst from his chest.

"Mrs. Nowell says there are all sorts of objects baked into this one," she whispered to him. "So be careful while you eat!"

"That I will," he replied in a low voice in her ear as Mrs. Nowell began to serve the pieces.

Margaret instantly began to cut hers into various bites, calling out, "a wishbone!" when she found what she was looking for.

"Ah," said Mr. Nowell, raising a finger in the air, "that is for luck."

"Your piece has a ring, Father!" Margaret exclaimed after searching through his slice of cake, and he grinned at how perfect it was.

"What did you find, Mrs. Nicholls?" she asked as Emily pulled something out of her mouth.

"An anchor," she said with a small smile.

"Ah," her mother said knowingly, "for safe harbor."

They went around the table reviewing all of the pieces found within the cake. As Charles looked at them all, their faces beautifully illuminated by the candlelight from the center of the table, he realized that never in his life had he truly known what it meant to be part of a family.

Family could take many forms, but these people had

taught him more in an hour than his own family had through his entire life.

"Thank you," he said, raising a glass of wine that Emily's father had poured, "for inviting my daughter and me into your home."

"Well, if you have Emily, you have all of us now for the rest of our lives," Teresa said with a laugh, "so welcome, Charles and Margaret."

They clinked glasses in the middle of the table, and with the plum pudding in front of them, the cheer of the cozy brick house, and the warmth of the people around the table, Charles finally found the Christmas spirit Emily had been telling about since the moment she had arrived in his life.

He leaned in next to her.

"Happy Christmas, Emily."

"Happy Christmas, Charles."

22

"Charles," Emily said the next morning as the family sat around the breakfast table. "What of all of the company awaiting you at your manor?"

Charles shrugged. "I have decided that I no longer care."

"Charles!"

"Well, why should I?" he asked. "They only come each Christmas to value what they believe will one day be theirs or to compare themselves to us. I believe it is time I begin a new tradition — by joining yours," he said to her. "From now on, we'll celebrate Christmas together here."

"But you always have your family through the holiday!" she exclaimed. "And your Twelfth Night party — oh dear, it's in just a few days."

"Perhaps we can continue with the party," he compromised, "but we will arrive here for Christmas."

Emily nodded, biting her lip. "My goodness, everything is changing so quickly."

"Are you not happy?" he asked before wishing he hadn't. He would prefer to hear her answer when it was just the two of them, and not in front of her entire family.

"Oh, I am," she said, giving him what she hoped was a reassuring smile as she squeezed his leg below the table. "It is just... Henrietta and Michael." She looked up at her family and explained, "Lord and Lady Coningsby's children. They are wonderful children, Charles, and I will so miss them. I also hate to leave them. How am I to know that their next governess will look after them well? They will feel as though I have disregarded them."

"You can always visit," Charles said reassuringly, "they do not live far."

"It will be rather strange," she mused, "to visit as Lady Doverton instead of their governess. My goodness, Lord and Lady Coningsby will be scandalized!"

Charles tilted his head for a moment, considering it. "They may be more understanding than you might think."

"I hope so."

"As for a governess for the children..."

They all turned in Teresa's direction as she spoke. "As it happens, I am looking for a position, and if they enjoyed their time with you, Emily, then perhaps they might be agreeable to as close as they can come?"

"Oh, Teresa, that would be wonderful!" Emily said, clapping her hands together. "Provided Lord and Lady Coningsby agree."

"I do not see why they wouldn't," Charles said with a shrug. "I am sure they would value your recommendation."

"They *are* fairly agreeable," Emily said. "Oh, how wonderful, Teresa."

"How wonderful for all of us!" Teresa exclaimed, and they all laughed.

Emily looked around the table, the smile on her face as warm as the happiness in her heart. How fearful she had been to enter Charles' manor but a few weeks ago. Now, her heart was full.

"What is it?" Charles asked, sensing her contemplation.

"It's a Christmas miracle."

~

DESPITE CHARLES' insistence on remaining with Emily's family as long as possible, soon enough it was time to return, as the Twelfth Night party would be taking place with or without them, and Emily finally convinced him that he could not shirk *all* of his responsibilities as earl.

"Besides," she said, smiling somewhat wickedly, "are you not anticipating the look on Edward's face when you inform him of Margaret's future inheritance?"

"Ah, yes," he said, the creases at the corner of his eyes growing with the size of his smile. "That just might make his visit this year worth it."

Emily laughed as the two of them and Margaret packed themselves into Charles' sleigh and began the short journey back to Ravenport. Thankfully, the air was somewhat warmer than when she had arrived at her parents' home, though that didn't stop her from needing to burrow into Charles for warmth — not that he seemed to mind.

"One other thing, Emily," he said, wrapping an arm around her, "I will have my physician travel to see your father the week after Christmastide concludes. His cough sounds near to pneumonia."

"It becomes worse each time I see him," she said gravely.

"We will do what we can to help him," he said, determination on his face. It seemed once Charles decided someone or something was under his care, he refused to be dissuaded from his goal.

"Thank you for going with me to see James' family," she said, turning to him. "I think they were pleased to know that I am in good hands."

"I can see why you joined their family," he said. "They are lovely people."

"I suppose I'd best change before I face your family again," Emily said as she pictured the drab work gown hidden beneath the layers of cloaks and blankets her mother had insisted they take with them.

"It doesn't matter," Charles said with a shrug. "Wear what you wish. They should know who you truly are, for that is the woman I fell in love with."

Emily smiled at him, though she hoped she was hiding the worry that was slowly rising within her.

As though he knew exactly what she was thinking, Charles spoke once more.

"It matters not what my family thinks of you. If they say anything disparaging, they can leave at once. They are here as my guests, and by extension, your guests as well. You're going to be the lady of the manor now, Emily. However you see fit to act in that role is fine with me, but one thing I will not have is anyone questioning it."

Emily nodded, setting her chin determinately.

Which was fortunate, for she was going to need all of that fortitude.

"Ah, Edward, I see you've made yourself at home," Charles said as he led Emily into the drawing room shortly after they had arrived. He looked over at Emily, worry on his face as he leaned in and asked her if she was still cold, but she smiled at him reassuringly.

"I'm fine, but thank you," she said. "See? My teeth have stopped chattering."

He nodded but pulled her close beside him as though to

warm her, a move that received the stare of the remainder of the room's occupants.

Edward was standing at the sideboard, pouring two glasses of brandy, one for himself and one for Thaddeus, as he ordered one of the footmen to bring a platter of pastries.

"Well, well, look who decided to return home," Edward said with a smirk. "Did you fetch your governess, Charles? I have but one question — were you aware that she was a governess before or after you chose her to pose as your bride?"

The rest of the room's occupants turned to them both in shock. Emily's cheeks warmed considerably, but Charles was ever the stoic Lord of Ravenport. Emily could see why he considered his emotionless demeanor to be an asset to his role. If none ever knew what was on his mind, then he felt it gave him an advantage. Perhaps it was not so conducive for a man attempting to better acquaint himself with his eight-year-old daughter but, in this case, it was opportune.

One corner of his lip curled as the ghost of a smile played upon it, and he languidly strode over to where Edward was standing, taking the decanter out of his hand and then pouring a drink of his own. He lifted his glass to Edward, Thaddeus, and then turned about the room.

"As my family is all currently present," he said, his gaze settling on Emily, who remained near the doorway, "I would like to invite you to our wedding. I have spoken with the minister, and we will be holding the ceremony as soon as the banns can be read, but before the Lenten season begins. So, if you are so inclined, you are welcome to return for the wedding in just over a month's time. Oh!" he held up a finger to add one more thing, and Emily tilted her head, curious as to what he might say.

"You are welcome to stay but one night. Then you will return home or find other lodgings."

His cousins stared at him, mouths agape, though none of them responded to his words. If Emily hadn't heard Charles herself, she would have thought that he was speaking a different language by how confused they all looked.

Emily bit the inside of her cheek as she attempted not to dissolve into laughter.

"But Charles," Edward said, holding his hands out wide in front of him, "this may be our *home* someday. I'm not sure what we ever did to deserve your ire."

"Allow me to first address your... misunderstandings," Charles said, crossing over to sit in one of the dainty pink chairs, where he looked elegantly masculine. "Edward, you act as though you are the Prince Regent himself when you do not even hold a title. Show some compassion, some respect for others, even if they are not of the noble set themselves. And get your son in line. If he compromises one of the maids, then he's marrying her, whether you like it or not. And," he stretched out the word as he took a sip of his drink. Emily could tell that he was enjoying this immensely. "Neither one of you will be the lord of this manor. In fact, there will not be a lord at all, but a lady."

Edward stalked toward him, his face mottled red in his fury.

"What are you on about, man?" he asked, his voice rising with each syllable. "Who else is going to inherit? Or is your mistress expecting already — despite her advanced age?"

"She is not my mistress," Charles said, completely calm, which only further infuriated Edward, though Emily guessed that was exactly Charles' intent. "She will be my wife in only a few weeks' time. Nor is she of advanced age. In fact, your own wife is significantly her elder."

Across the room, Leticia began a protest, but Charles ignored her.

"To answer your question, no, she is not expecting a child. It is my daughter who will inherit."

Gasps resounded around the room before a slow murmur arose.

"I must wait for the solicitor to review the documents, but if I properly understand what I am reading, then the line passes through *any* child of mine — not just a son."

"This is ludicrous!" Edward exclaimed, but Charles simply shrugged and lifted a pastry from the platter that a footman had placed on the table between them all and placed it in his mouth.

"Mmm, delicious," he said then held one out to Emily. "Here, darling, you must try one."

Edward snorted and turned away, bracing his hands upon the sideboard. "Guests will be arriving at any moment."

"Ah, yes," Charles said, rising now. "It is time to determine our roles for the evening. Toller?"

His butler came in dutifully, his hands full.

"A card for each of you," he said with a smile, for he and Emily both knew what they held for each of the room's inhabitants. "I look forward to tonight."

IT WAS *QUITE* THE EVENING — one Charles would remember for the rest of his life. They had always had a Twelfth Night celebration, but this was different from any he had ever celebrated before. His cousins retired to bed as early as could possibly be considered even promptly polite.

"Perhaps," Emily said, as she and Charles sat together on the sofa in front of the fire, the only ones left awake in the early hours of the morning, "their departure had something to do with the characters they were forced to play for the evening."

"You don't think Edward enjoyed his?" Charles asked with a laugh.

"Hmm," Emily said, bringing one long finger to her beautiful plush lips. "I do not think I shall ever, for the rest of my life, forget the image of him standing there in his costume announcing himself, "Take Joe Giber, the king's jester, he's the fellow for your yoke, Tho' marriage, it must be confess'd, by most wits is counted no joke.' I think the best part of it all was that you made Toller the King for the night," Emily said with a chuckle.

As was often the custom, the servants had taken part for this night only. They had seemed slightly nervous at first but quickly joined in the revelry.

"And best of all?" Charles said, the lines surrounding his eyes relaxing. "By tomorrow evening, they will all be gone. We will say farewell to them as we will to the greenery and all of the Christmas decor. Which will leave you and me."

"Although I really don't think that you and I should remain alone here at Ravenport," Emily said, worrying her bottom lip, and Charles nodded.

"I agree on that," he said, "which is why I have asked your family to come to visit until after the wedding."

"Truly?" A wide smile broke out on her face. "Thank you, Charles."

"Anything," he said, resting his chin on top of her head as she snuggled in toward him.

"Now, what do you say we go see if there is any leftover Twelfth Night cake?"

"I think that is a wonderful idea," she said, working up her courage. "But first..."

She tilted her head to look up toward him, shifting her body so that she was straddling him. She took his face in her hands, then leaned in and placed her lips upon his. She was hesitant, unsure of how to go forward when *she* was the aggressor. But her invitation was all he needed, and whether he sensed her hesitation or not, he soon took over, ravaging her lips with his. His strong fingers kneaded the back of her head, ridding her of all of the pins that held her chignon in place. Soon her long hair was floating about her shoulders, and she felt a surge of power rise within her as she leaned down toward him. He wanted her. Her, Emily Nicholls. And not only as his mistress, as a woman to enjoy himself with, but as his wife.

When he finally walked her through the estate to lead her up to her bedroom, he stopped under the entrance to the saloon.

"What do you say we put this mistletoe to good use one last time before it's gone for the year?" he asked, a gleam in his eye.

"I would say that is a very fine idea, indeed," Emily said with a chuckle, and when she leaned up to kiss him, she let out a startled yelp when his arms came around her and practically bent her over backward as he bestowed on her a kiss that she thought only occurred in one's dreams.

"Thank you," he said when he finally set her back down.

"I think I should be thanking you," she said with a laugh.

"No," he shook his head. "Thank *you* for coming and turning this empty estate into a home. For reuniting me with my daughter. For showing me that Christmas is a time to celebrate family and all that we are fortunate to have in life. That duty and responsibility are not everything and one needs more to live a proper life. I love you, Emily."

"And I you, Charles."

EPILOGUE

Eleven months later

"Sit, if you please."

Emily and Charles dutifully sat next to one another on the long blue sofa that lined the wall of the music room. It had become the perfect place from where she and Charles could enjoy Margaret's frequent concerts.

They shared a small smile as Margaret, her stature seemingly so tiny behind the massive pianoforte, stood and addressed them.

"As we will soon be leaving for Newport, I thought it best I share my Christmas gift with you before we departed."

She sat primly, cleared her throat, and then the melody began flowing out of her lips and her fingers. She sang of Christmas, of family, and of the love that wrapped around them all.

Charles wordlessly handed Emily his handkerchief to wipe the tears flowing down her face, but after a quick look beside her, Emily handed it back so that he could wipe his own eyes.

When she finished, they both sat there, stunned for a moment, before rising as one and clapping for the little girl.

"That was most beautiful, Margaret," Emily said, the first to regain her composure.

It represented everything that their family meant, all that had brought them together, and what the future would hold for them all.

"You will have to play it again when we reach Emily's parents' house," Charles said with a watery smile, "for I know they will love it as much as we do."

"Of course," she said, and when she rounded the piano and Charles held his arms out, she went willingly, rushing into them to accept his embrace. Emily held a hand over her heart at the love that was now freely expressed between father and daughter. What would have happened to the little girl without knowing how much her father cared for her, Emily wasn't sure, but she was happy beyond measure that Margaret knew just how much she meant to him.

She was equally grateful for her own father's health. Charles' physician had proved somewhat of a miracle worker, and while her father's lungs would never fully recover, they were beginning to heal.

"Now," Emily said, "I have a surprise for you."

"You do?" Margaret said, looking up at her with wide eyes.

"I do," Emily confirmed, holding out her hand. "Have you ever made plum pudding?"

"No," Margaret said with a shake of her head. "Have you, Father?"

"I have not," he responded with a wink. "But it looks like we're both going to be learning how today."

They trekked down to the kitchen, where the cook greeted them with a smile. Emily had forewarned her of their disruption of her kitchen today, and besides that, Mrs. Graydon had now thankfully found another position and would no longer be attempting to impose her will.

Charles watched as Emily and Margaret sifted the various ingredients into the bowl, and then finally it was time to stir.

"Very well, Margaret," she said. "Why don't you stir first? Clockwise now, and while you stir, be sure to make a wish."

She handed her the wooden spoon, and the girl dutifully closed her eyes and swirled the pudding.

"Charles?"

He nodded, took the spoon, and did as he was bid.

"Your turn, Emily," Margaret said, and Emily nodded, smiling as she made her wish.

When she opened her eyes, she found that Margaret was watching her expectantly from where she sat perched on the edge of the counter, her legs dangling over the edge.

"What did you wish for?" Margaret asked.

"Well, I should not be telling my wish, should I?" Emily responded with a laugh, but Margaret's serious expression remained.

"Did you wish that you would have children? And you, Father, did you wish for a son?"

"Oh, sweetheart," Emily said, leaning on the counter so that she could look directly at Margaret from the same level. "I can tell you with all assurance that was not my wish. If we are to ever be blessed with more children, then we will welcome them into our family, of course. However, if we do not, then I am perfectly happy having you in my life. I know I will never be your mother, but since she is gone, I will be the next best thing."

Margaret nodded sagely, and when her teeth sucked in her bottom lip, Emily knew she was trying hard not to allow her smile to show.

"It matters not to me whether or not I have a son," Charles said, walking over to the counter and taking Margaret's hand. "We have each other, and that is what truly matters."

Margaret beamed now and then raised her hands for Charles to help her down from the counter.

"Can I go ask Cook for one of her pastries now?"

Emily smiled at her enthusiasm, and at how all she had needed was a bit of assurance for her smile to return. She supposed it would take a good deal of love to erase her mother's repeated insistence that her father cared nothing for her.

Charles wrapped an arm around Emily's waist as they both looked on after Margaret who took a pastry and started upstairs.

"Did you mean that?" he asked, turning her in his arms to face him. "Are you happy?"

"I am happier than words could ever express," she said with a smile as he took her hand and began leading her out of the kitchen and up the stairs.

"Because it's Christmas again?" he teased.

"Here's the thing, Charles," she said as she looked up at him, "Every day is Christmas when I'm with you."

"And this year there is one gift that is better than any other," he said. "We do not have to spend the entire season with my family."

"Though they will be coming for the Twelfth Night party," she reminded him.

"Yes, I do wish you hadn't convinced me of that."

"They are still your family, Charles," she said. "It would be wrong to not see them at all."

"Would it, though?" he asked with a sigh, and she laughed at his dramatics.

"Well, you can always dress Edward up as the jester again if that would make you feel better."

"Actually," he said, an eager smile brightening his face, "it would."

And as they laughed, their hands joined together and their daughter full of spirit in front of them, Emily's heart had never felt so full.

And she knew that whatever came their way, they would face it. Together.

"Father, Emily," Margaret said as she turned around with a grin. "Look what Toller and I put up this morning."

Emily looked up to where Margaret was pointing.

"Mistletoe," Emily said, an eyebrow arched as she looked over at Charles.

"We'd best not waste it," he said winking at her, allowing the man he had hidden inside to emerge.

He leaned in, kissed her long and hard, and Emily knew that his very being was the greatest gift she could ever ask for. A gift that lasted all year long.

For Charles had given her what she had always wanted but, for years now, had never thought would be her reality — a family of her own.

~

THE END

~

DUKE OF CHRISTMAS

SEARCHING HEARTS PREQUEL

PREVIEW
the first story of the Harrington family with Lionel and
Marie...

1

1784

"Whatever do you mean, Jane, he has a taste for depravity?"

Marie Colemore stared at her friend as horror began to churn in her belly, along with another emotion she couldn't quite identify, but it seemed something akin to excitement. According to Jane, her closest friend, Marie's intended fiancé, a man who was not only one of the most powerful dukes in England but one of the richest, had tendencies of which one should never discuss. Surely that was not something to be particularly excited about. But at least, finally, she was learning something about him — something more than could be found in Debrett's. And perhaps, she had found a way out. The man hadn't shown a glimmer of interest in her and, in fact, had outright ignored her. Now she knew why.

"I only mean..." Jane looked around her furtively, to ensure that no prying ears could overhear their conversation. "My brother — you know he has always had a particular fondness for you, Marie — mentioned to me that perhaps you should be aware of the duke's particular ... proclivities."

Marie took her friend by the wrist and pulled her from the crowded ballroom, looking one way and another before finally choosing an open door. Once they were through the entrance, the door closed behind them, Marie released Jane and made her way over to the carved giltwood mint green settee, taking the seat closest to the roaring fire in the hearth.

"Tell me more," she demanded, and Jane, her oldest friend, as blonde and tall as Marie was dark and small, took a seat across from her, primly sitting on the edge of the matching Chippendale side chair.

"My brother went to school with the duke, you know — to Eton. They have been friends since childhood, and the duke drew acquaintances to him easily, with his charm and his title. It is not often a current duke finds himself at school, but then, that is what his father had wanted."

Marie knew the Duke of Ware's father had died when he was quite young, and he had practically grown up with the title. Unlike some, however, who frittered away the wealth and responsibility received at a young age, he had always seemed rather respectable — responsible, even, keeping his name out of the scandal sheets.

"Anyway," Jane continued. "Already having the responsibility that came along with the title, the duke decided for himself that he couldn't go about causing scandal with young ladies as many of the other young men did. Oh, he had a good time to be sure, but he didn't want to make his activities as public as some others did. He already had a great deal within business investments and that sort of thing."

"I understand and know all that," said Marie, impatient for Jane to get to the heart of the matter. She had made it a priority to search for information on the movements of the man she would one day marry, despite his persistent denial of her. "Carry on."

"Right," Jane said with a nod, and she twisted her hands in her lap. "You know, of course, that the duke is an attractive man..."

Marie nodded. Of course she knew that. She had met him on occasion, but that had been years prior. She hadn't spoken to him in ages — since his father had died. He had been a very young man, while she was still a child. It seemed that in his will, the former Duke of Ware had expressed an interest in his son being married to the daughter of his oldest friend, a friend he knew would raise his children with the utmost propriety. It was true that Marie's parents, the Marquess and Marchioness of St. James, had ensured in recent years that their children learned to be acceptable members of society, but they had allowed Marie a great deal of freedom in her youth. When her mother tried to harness all of that energy to raise her daughter to become a respectable bride, it was, perhaps, slightly too late. For by that time, Marie had ideas of her own, and her mother now despaired, believing it was her own fault the duke so blatantly ignored her daughter.

"Well, it seems," Jane said in a whisper now, though the room was empty save the two of them, "he began frequenting a brothel, as did many other young men, of course. But then the *madame* took an interest in him, and he in her. And then—"

"While I am enjoying your tale, Lady Jane, I must say that you are getting some details wrong."

Jane let out a yelp of fright, while Marie whirled around

in her seat to the direction of the voice, with its deep, rich tone that sent chills down her spine. She searched in the shadows to see who was speaking but saw no one — until the figure stepped out into the light.

Her heart stopped. It couldn't be.

But yes, of course, with the way her luck continually seemed to turn, it was.

"Lady Marie," he said, sauntering over to the settee where she sat frozen, despite the heat thrown by the fire beside her. Her eyes locked on his as he bent over her hand, picking up her fingers and bringing his lips to the back of it. "How lovely to see you again. You look beautiful, as always."

"Th-thank you, your grace," she said, finally pulling her eyes from his to look at Jane, who sat on her chair with her mouth wide open.

"Tell me, Lady Jane," he said, straightening, though he didn't let go of Marie's hand. "How fares your brother? It has been some time since I have seen my dear ... *friend*. You will have to give him my regards. Now, would you give me a moment alone with my betrothed?"

Jane squeaked out something unintelligible but looked at Marie, who gave her a nod, telling her she would be fine. It was improper, true, but what was the worst that could happen at this point?

So this was his bride.

Lionel took his time perusing her from head to toe, and she knew it, too — she squirmed in discomfort but didn't take her eyes from his, and he was impressed that she didn't shy away from him. Though not his type — no innocent lady was — she had the look of a little vixen, her dark, jet black hair piled high on her head, her shockingly crystal blue eyes staring back at him from a face that would make a sculptor's fingers itch.

He leaned down toward her, running the pad of his thumb over the soft skin of her cheek. She jumped a bit but didn't lean back.

"Was what Jane said true?" she asked boldly, her eyes searching his, and he raised his eyebrows at her.

"Do you want to know?"

"Of course I do," she answered, straightening her shoulders.

"Very well, then," he said, smiling at her as he sat in the chair Jane had vacated, the wood creaking from his weight. He certainly was a big man, his shoulders broad and his chest wide. "Some of it is true, yes. I have certain tendencies that I enjoy, but nothing out of the ordinary. Besides, there is nothing for you to be frightened of. I should not expect you to fulfill those needs — unless you want to, that is."

She finally broke her gaze away from him, looking at the floor, the only sign of her reaction to him the twitching of her fingers.

"You will fill those needs elsewhere, then, is that the case?" she asked, meeting his stare again, her chin set resolutely.

"I suppose that is what I had thought to do, yes," he said with a shrug. "I find that seems to work well for most married couples."

Marie sat still for a moment before leaning forward in her chair.

"I don't think I altogether like that idea," she said matter-of-factly, and he raised an eyebrow, though inside he was smiling at the thought that she was already becoming possessive of him. In fact, he rather liked it.

He leaned forward, picking up a long strand of her dark hair from where it framed her face, curling it around his finger.

"Don't do that," she said, wrinkling her nose as she swatted his hand away.

"Do what, my sweet?" he asked, bringing his face closer to hers.

"Touch me," she said, though she didn't move away. "And I am not your sweet."

"No?" he asked softly, his lips now but a breath away from hers. "Was I misinformed? Are you not Lady Marie Colemore, daughter of the Marquess of St. James, who my father was so insistent on me marrying?"

"Yes, but—"

"Then, you are my sweet."

"But—"

He silenced her protestations as he leaned in and took her lips with his. She was to be his wife — why not have a taste? He could sense her shock as she stilled for a moment, but she didn't sit back, didn't push him away. Lionel didn't force anything further on her for the moment, but simply allowed her to enjoy the sensation of what might very well be her first kiss, before he began moving his lips over hers, at first softly, but slowly growing in force. He leaned over her now before gently pulling her up toward him, wrapping his arms around her, and twining the fingers of one hand into her hair.

When the tip of his tongue teased the seal of her lips, she opened to him with a bit of a moan, sinking into him, and he held her even closer. He didn't know how long he stood there kissing her, tasting her, but eventually, desperation for her overcame all else as he wanted her in more ways than would be proper to act upon with his betrothed in a drawing room at the home of one of the *ton*'s leading peers.

He eased back from her, leaving a kiss on her forehead, before placing her back on the settee and returning to his chair as he watched her with a smile on his face. Her shock wore off quickly, soon to be replaced by a fierce attack on him.

"Why did you do that?" she demanded, to which he laughed.

"Because I wanted to. You liked it, didn't you, sweet?"

"I'm not your sweet."

"You are now, love."

"Or your love — *your grace*."

"My, aren't we formal for a couple that is going to become so intimate so soon, are we not, Marie? Call me by my given name, will you?"

"And that is?"

He was a bit surprised she didn't know, given that they had been pledged to be married for some time now, despite the fact they had hardly spoken.

"Lionel."

"Your name is Lionel?"

"It is," he said, wanting to laugh at the incredulous expression on her face. "Do you not approve?"

"It's simply ... not what I expected," she said, shrugging one delicate shoulder. "It wouldn't be my first choice, no, but I suppose it will have to do."

He did laugh now, wondering how this woman, the daughter of a marquess, spoke so openly of what she thought, unlike the typical lady of her class. She would keep him on his toes, to be sure — when the time came to wed, that is. "Well, you will have to take it up with my mother, I suppose, as she was the one who chose it."

"You wouldn't tell her!" Marie exclaimed, turning wide eyes on him, and he chucked her chin softly.

"No, I'm just teasing you," he said. "Of course I wouldn't tell her. It will be difficult enough to wrest control of the household away from her once we marry. I shouldn't want to make it worse."

"What do you mean?" she asked, her eyes narrowing now. "You believe it will be difficult for me to get along with your mother?"

"Most likely," he said nonchalantly. "She has been running my house and my life since I was fifteen. When I fully took on my duties as a duke, I left her to continue managing the household as she wished."

"I see," said Marie, biting her lip. "I have to say, your gr — Lionel, I am beginning to think this situation is not altogether ideal."

"No?"

"No," she said with additional resolution, standing and beginning to pace, her lips turned in a frown. "In fact, I think this is all a huge mistake. I will speak to my father tonight and tell him to call this entire thing off. I do not want to be married to a man who has already decided he will take other women to bed, meanwhile leaving me in a house with a woman who only wishes ill of me!"

"Very well," he said, crossing one leg over the other, enjoying watching her stride back and forth over the carpet with such force, he thought she would wear right through it. "I shall find another wife, then. It shouldn't be overly difficult. When the will was read, it seemed you would do well enough because of your lineage and your dowry, and I figured it didn't make much of a difference, so why not? I am thirty now, so I suppose at some time I should actually consider marriage to a respectable lady who will provide me with an heir. But if you're opposed to the idea, I will speak to the solicitor tomorrow and arrange everything to be called off."

She stopped pacing and stared at him, her mouth agape.

"That's it? You really don't care?"

"I do not."

"You ... you ingrate!"

And with that, she whirled around on her heel and stormed out of the room, slamming the door in her wake.

DUKE OF CHRISTMAS is now available for purchase on Amazon.

ALSO BY ELLIE ST. CLAIR

ABOUT THE AUTHOR

 Ellie has always loved reading, writing, and history. For many years she has written short stories, non-fiction, and has worked on her true love and passion -- romance novels.

In every era there is the chance for romance, and Ellie enjoys exploring many different time periods, cultures, and geographic locations. No matter when or where, love can always prevail. She has a particular soft spot for the bad boys of history, and loves a strong heroine in her stories.

She enjoys walks under the stars with her own prince charming, as well as spending time at the lake with her children, and running with her Husky/Border Collie cross.

www.prairielilypress.com/ellie-st-clair
ellie@prairielilypress.com

Made in the USA
Columbia, SC
03 December 2019

84265924R00136